Note to Readers

While the Harringtons and their friends are fictional, the events they experienced actually happened. In 1935, the United States was still experiencing the Great Depression. Swarms of grasshoppers and other insects destroyed many crops that managed to survive harsh growing conditions. Unemployment was still high, and many people couldn't find work.

The kidnapping of nine-year-old George Weyerhaeuser took place, as did the baseball school with Tubby Graves. And the political events in Asia and Europe affected how some people viewed their Japanese and Italian neighbors.

For many Americans, 1935 was a year for starting over. Like the Harringtons, they left their homes and moved west, hoping for a better life.

STARTING OVER

Susan Martins Miller

PUBLISHING, INC.
Uhrichsville, Ohio

© MCMXCVIII by Barbour Publishing, Inc.

ISBN 1-57748-509-2

Published by Barbour Publishing, Inc., P.O. Box 719, Uhrichsville, Ohio 44683
http://www.barbourbooks.com

ecpa Member of the
Evangelical Christian
Publishers Association

Printed in the United States of America.

Cover illustration by Peter Pagano.
Inside illustrations by Adam Wallenta.

CHAPTER 1

Counting Pennies

Isabel eyed her dark-haired brother as they trudged home from school. The wide Minneapolis street in front of them was nearly irresistible. Traces of a late winter snow littered the sidewalk, sloshing under their feet as they walked. The day was cool enough to need a coat but sunny enough to make Isabel glad to be out of school for the afternoon.

Steven was thirteen. Isabel was only ten. His legs were long and lanky, and he prided himself on how well he ran the bases of a baseball diamond. But she was tall for her age and ran pretty fast herself. And she knew Steven could not resist a dare.

"I'll race you!" she shouted and spurted out in front of him.

Isabel knew that looking back would slow her down, so she did not turn her head to see what Steven was doing. But she heard his footsteps pounding behind her. Grinning, she sprang forward even faster. One hand gripped the strap that tied her small bundle of books together. Her curly dark hair swirled around her face. She thundered down the sidewalk with Steven at her heels. Only two more blocks and they would be home.

"Can't catch me!" she called out gleefully without turning around.

Steven was nudging her from behind. Isabel concentrated on her feet and moved them even faster. She pulled a step ahead, then two. Soon they clambered up the front steps side by side and crashed, breathless, through the front door.

"I win!" Isabel declared as she flung herself into the sofa. Her brown eyes gleamed with victory. Her chest heaved as she tried to catch her breath.

"Only because you don't have as many books as I do," Steven countered. He tossed his book bundle into a chair to prove his point. It was much heavier than her own, Isabel had to admit. Despite his protest, Steven's blue eyes sparkled with the pleasure of running.

Footsteps on the bare wood floor made Isabel turn toward the stairs. Seven-year-old Frank and five-year-old Audrey tumbled down. They clattered into the front room.

"It's mine! Give it back," Frank insisted. His eyes, blue like his brother's, glowed with indignation. He brushed his straight blond hair out of his face with a grimy hand.

"I'm just looking at it," Audrey answered. "I'm not hurting it."

"What are you two fighting over now?" Steven asked.

"She has my truck," Frank said angrily, "and I want it back."

"I can see that," Steven said. He turned to his little sister. She clutched a white metal truck with the Coca-Cola logo painted brightly on the side. It was Frank's prize possession. "Audrey, that truck belongs to Frank. Did you ask his permission to play with it?"

Audrey hung her head and stuck out her lower lip. Tears formed in her dark eyes. "I'm just looking at it. I'm not going to break it."

"I know you won't break it," Steven answered. "But it belongs to Frank. You must ask his permission to borrow it." Gently he pried the truck out of Audrey's clutch and handed it to Frank.

Audrey stared at her shoes, with her wavy dark hair bouncing around her face. "May I borrow your truck?" she mumbled.

Frank tucked the truck under his arm. Steven gave Frank a look that said, *She asked politely, now you answer politely.*

"In a few minutes," Frank said grudgingly.

"How many minutes?" Audrey wanted to know.

"Ten."

Audrey turned to Isabel. "How long is ten minutes?"

"Not long," Isabel assured the little girl.

"Bel-bel," said a tiny voice. One-year-old Barbara had toddled into the room, followed closely by her twin brother, Ed. Their dark heads bobbed as they both climbed up into Isabel's lap. "Bel-bel."

"Yes, Bel-bel is here," Isabel said, "home from school. What are you two doing up from your nap so soon?" Barbie rubbed one eye with a tiny fist and stared at Isabel.

"She's still tired," Steven observed, "Eddie, too." He scooped up his small brother from Isabel's lap and gently thumped his tiny nose.

7

"Where's Mama?" Isabel wondered. She turned her head toward the kitchen. "Let's go say hello to Mama."

Walking through the doorway into the kitchen, Isabel found her mother sitting at the kitchen table with a scrap of paper and a small pile of coins. Her straight blond hair was tucked behind her ears. Mother's lips moved silently as she counted the money, pushing the coins to one side two at a time. Isabel waited until the counting was over before she spoke. She hated it when she was interrupted while counting, so she did not want to interrupt her mother. Her mother's blue eyes squinted at the coins as she counted. At last she was done. She wrote a number at the bottom of her scrap of paper.

"Mama, we're home," Isabel said.

Mama turned to her middle daughter and smiled. "I thought I heard a ruckus in the front room."

"That was Frank and Audrey," Isabel explained.

Mama sighed. "They've been scrapping all day. I haven't had time to take them out for some real exercise."

"I guess Frank is feeling all right, then," Isabel said.

Mama nodded. "I kept him home from school because I thought he was coming down with a cold again, but he hasn't acted sick for a moment since breakfast."

"I'm glad," Isabel said. "He's been sick so much this winter."

"I'm just glad I didn't have to call the doctor again," Mama said. "He's been so patient with us, but his family needs to eat, too."

Isabel knew her parents still owed the doctor money from the time Frank had had bronchitis at Christmastime, nearly three months ago.

Mama had turned her attention back to her coins.

"Are you going shopping?" Isabel asked. She set Barbara down on the floor and handed her a wooden spoon to play with.

"I need a few things for supper," Mama answered.

Mama did not say what Isabel knew, that she was counting the coins to see if she had enough money to feed her rambunctious family that evening. Isabel had seen her mother do this before, especially toward the end of the month. Daddy would be paid again soon, but would it be soon enough?

"Did Steven come in with you?" Mama asked.

Isabel nodded.

Mama called her oldest son, and he soon appeared. He put Eddie down next to Barbara. The twins slapped at each other playfully. Isabel gently removed the wooden spoon from Barbara's grip before she could swing it at her twin.

"Steven, I want you to go down to the grocer's," Mama said. "I've made a very careful list. If you stick to what I've written down, you should be able to pay for it."

Steven picked up the scrap of paper. "What are we having tonight?"

"Casserole."

"Potatoes and green beans again?" Steven groaned.

"There's a lot of nutrition in potatoes," his mother answered, "especially if you leave the skins on. And they fill you up."

"I wish I could fill up on a nice thick slice of fried ham."

Isabel saw a cloud pass over her mother's face. The family rarely had meat with their evening meal. It was simply too costly to buy meat for the whole family, even in small portions. But Mama did not let on.

"I'm saving a dab of butter for your biscuit tonight," Mama told Steven. "And you can have extra milk with your oatmeal in the morning."

Steven gave a thin smile. Despite his desire for better food, he knew his mother was doing the best she could. He looked at the list. "So you just want flour, six eggs, and milk?"

Mama nodded. "I think that will get us through to Friday."

Payday, Isabel thought to herself. Steven left for the grocer's.

"Where's Alice?" Isabel asked about her fifteen-year-old sister, the oldest child in the Harrington family.

"She's working today," Mama answered. "Mr. Burton said he could use her."

"But it's not Saturday." Alice had been working every Saturday at the pharmacy for almost a year, cleaning and stocking shelves. Every month, she gave her paycheck to Mama.

"Alice is going to start working on Wednesdays after school as well as Saturdays," Mama explained. "Mr. Burton offered her the extra hours. The extra money will help. And jobs are hard to find these days. She didn't want to turn him down and have him look for someone else."

Isabel felt a familiar sinking feeling in her stomach. "Mama, when is the depression going to be over? Alice says that things weren't always this way, that Minneapolis used to be a good place to live."

"Minneapolis is still a good place to live," Mama assured Isabel. She moved to the sink and began rinsing the dishes that had been sitting there since breakfast. "Our families are here, and we're grateful your father still has a job at the Pillsbury mill. It's a beautiful part of America."

"But Alice says it's not the same as it was when she was little," Isabel said. "She used to get new dresses and have birthday parties."

Mama sighed. "I'll be honest. It wasn't always as bad as it has been the last few years. But I didn't come from a rich family, either. My father came from Germany and struggled to make a living. During the war, it wasn't easy for German-Americans to keep their jobs. Grandpa Schmidt worked very hard but didn't make much money. The important thing was that I came from a happy family—and so do you."

"I know, Mama. You're right."

"God has taken care of us this far," Mama said. "He's not going to abandon us now."

Audrey appeared in the kitchen and set her hands on her hips. "Has it been ten minutes yet?"

Isabel glanced at the clock. "Yes, it's been ten minutes."

Audrey wheeled around and screamed, "Frank! It's ten minutes."

Isabel followed her sister to the front room, where Frank was happily rolling his truck on the wooden floor.

"Audrey," Isabel said, "remember what Steven said about asking politely?"

Audrey put on her most angelic face. "Frank, may I please play with your truck now?" she asked sweetly.

Frank hesitated just a moment before answering, "Okay, you can have a turn. But I want it back!"

Triumphantly Audrey picked up the truck and scampered up to her bedroom. Frank sprawled on the floor and did not move.

"Frank, do you feel all right?" Isabel asked. She thought he looked pale.

"I'm tired," he answered without turning his head toward her.

Maybe Mama is right after all, Isabel thought. *Maybe Frank is getting sick again.*

Isabel moved to the big window and looked out. In the distance, she could see the smoke rising from the Pillsbury mills. Those flour mills had given jobs to thousands of people over the years. Right now her father was lucky enough to be one of the employees. He had gone to college and learned how to design the equipment that kept the mills in business.

Isabel liked to visit the mills because she liked to watch the river that ran through the heart of Minneapolis. She had seen pictures from the old days, when only a few bridges spanned the river and people walked across or perhaps took a horse and carriage. Trolleys had filled the streets, and trains from east and west brought goods and people to Minneapolis. The trains were still there, of course. But not so many people rode the trolleys. Now there were cars. Many of the cars were old because not very many people could afford to buy new ones. Daddy had kept their 1925 Chrysler running for ten years now.

Steven would be at the grocer's by now, Isabel thought. He would be standing at the counter telling Mr. Berg what he wanted and counting out the coins carefully. He would do his best to bring some change home to Mama, even if only a few pennies.

"Bel-bel."

Isabel looked down to see Barbie wrapping her arms around her big sister's leg. She picked up the baby and nuzzled her face against the soft, smooth skin of Barbara's face. "You're lucky to be little," Isabel told her sister. "I hope that when you're my age, Mama won't be counting pennies for milk."

CHAPTER 2

The Accident

"Has anyone seen the newspaper?" Steven asked on Saturday morning as he finished his breakfast. He pushed his empty oatmeal bowl toward the center of the kitchen table.

"I don't think anyone has even had a chance to bring it in," Mama said. She stooped to wipe Eddie's chin before any more juice dripped onto his only clean shirt.

"I'll get it!" Audrey volunteered, and she zoomed through the house to the front porch. Standing near the kitchen door, Isabel watched her.

Frank lay on the couch, playing quietly with Barbara. Isabel did not think that Frank looked very well. He was not

13

hungry for breakfast. He had barely glanced up when Audrey noisily charged through the room. And Isabel had seen the concern in her mother's face that morning as she touched Frank's forehead.

"Why is Daddy working today?" Isabel asked. "I thought he was supposed to have this weekend off."

"He was," Mama answered. She began wiping the table clean. "But there was a problem with one of the machines. Since Daddy helped to design it, they thought he might have some ideas for fixing it."

"Daddy can fix anything," Isabel said.

Mama smiled. "Well, perhaps not absolutely everything. But he has a good understanding of how machines work."

"Did he find that rattle in the car?" Steven wanted to know.

"He says it's fixed," Mama answered.

"It's a really old car."

"We're lucky to have any car at all," Mama said, "especially one big enough for a family of nine."

The family car was a 1925 Chrysler B-70. Isabel had heard the story dozens of times of how Mama and Daddy had decided they needed a car when Isabel, their third child, was born. They wanted the biggest one they could find because they wanted more children. Daddy had talked the salesman into selling him the Chrysler for $1,550. Over the years, the car had filled up with the Harrington children who followed Isabel.

Steven was right. It was an old car. But Daddy kept it polished as if it were still brand new. Its gray coating and black roof gleamed in the sunlight. The running boards along the sides merged smoothly into the fenders that rose over the sleek wheels. The long hood hinted at the powerful engine hidden underneath. Even though the family had seven children, the car had barely a scratch on it.

"Here's the paper." Audrey plopped the newspaper in front of Steven and leaned her elbows on the table to watch his next move. Steven turned directly to the sports section.

"What does it say?" Audrey asked.

"Well, let's see. It says that Minneapolis should have a good baseball season this year," Steven reported. "The coaches are very hopeful that the team will learn to work together and put out a good showing."

"They say that every year," Isabel commented. She was not impressed.

"But this could really be the year," Steven said.

"What else does it say?" Audrey persisted.

"Wow, look at this," Steven said excitedly. "There's a rowing team at the University of Washington that might go to the Olympics next year."

"The University of Washington?" Isabel asked. "That's a million miles from here."

"Actually only about two thousand, in Seattle," Steven corrected. "I wish I could go to the Olympics."

"You're not good enough for that," Isabel said.

Steven rolled his eyes. "I mean just to watch, silly, not to compete."

"What about that runner you're always talking about?" Mama asked. She turned on the faucet and ran water into the sink to wash dishes.

"Do you mean Jesse Owens?"

"That's the one."

"There's nothing about him today. But they would be crazy not to send him to Berlin for the Olympics next year. He's the fastest man alive."

"Down!" Eddie demanded. Satisfied that his face and hands were free of food and he could not smear anything on

15

the wall, his mother lifted him out of the wooden high chair and set him on the floor. Immediately he toddled toward the front room in search of his twin.

"Mama, can I go out today?" Isabel asked.

"Out where?"

Isabel shrugged. "Just out."

Mama's blue eyes twinkled. "Are you planning to go off in search of an adventure today?"

Isabel smiled. "Maybe. Do you want to come along?"

"That depends. What would we do?"

The spark in her mother's eye told Isabel to let her imagination run free.

"First, we would sneak downtown and into the mill to say hello to Daddy. No one would see us because we would flatten ourselves against the walls and hold our breath whenever anyone came near."

"Like this?" Mama sucked in her breath and pressed herself against the kitchen wall. Water dripped from the dishrag she still held in her hand.

"Yes. And then we would creep into Daddy's office and take him a surprise."

"What would it be?"

"German chocolate cake. He loves that."

"Yes, he does. He tells me he married me for my German chocolate cake."

"But we're not supposed to be at the mill, so we have to sneak out. Only we can't go back the way we came in because now there are people there."

Mama gave a gasp. "What will we do?"

"We'll curl up into small balls and roll down the back hall. They'll think we're machine parts or something. When we get to the stairs, we'll run down them three at a time, so fast that no one can catch us. They won't even know it's us."

"Whew!" Mama acted relieved. "And then what?"

"Then we'll crawl under the bridge and watch St. Anthony Falls."

"Won't that be cold?"

Isabel shook her head. "We won't care. We'll just be glad to be out in the sun and the wind. We won't come home until bedtime."

"How about suppertime?"

"We won't be hungry."

"What about the rest of the family?"

"Well, all right, we'll come home for supper."

Mama tousled Isabel's dark hair. "That would be a delightful way to spend the day," she said. "I would rather do that than spend all day doing laundry."

Isabel knew what her mother was going to say next. "But if we don't do the laundry, who will?"

"That's right," Mama said sadly. "I really need you to help with the children today. Your father hasn't got a single clean shirt left to wear to church tomorrow."

Isabel glanced at her brother, still immersed in the sports page. "What about Steven?"

"Don't you worry about that," Mama said. "I've got a list for Steven as well."

"Aw, Mama, it's a nice day," Steven groaned. "I was going to find some guys and play ball."

"Maybe this afternoon you can both go out," Mama said. "Right now, I need your help around here. Your father and Alice are both working, so I'm depending on you."

"What do you want us to do?" Isabel asked.

"Steven, I want you to see if you can fix the loose banister halfway up the stairs. I'm afraid one of the other children will

17

fall through it. Isabel, I'd like you to try to keep the twins out of trouble and keep an eye on Frank. He doesn't look well to me."

"Are you going to call the doctor?" Isabel asked.

Mama shook her head. "Not just yet. We'll see how he is tonight."

Steven scraped his chair back. "I'll need some tools from the shed."

Isabel reached out a hand for Audrey. "Come on, Audrey, let's go play with the twins."

"If Frank is sick, can I play with his truck?" Audrey asked.

"You have to ask Frank that question," Isabel answered.

In the front room, she looked around at the clutter. No matter how often Mama straightened things up, seven children in the house meant that there was always something that needed to be put away.

"Let's surprise Mama and clean up the house," Isabel suggested.

"I'm too little. I'm five," Audrey answered.

"Five is big enough," Isabel insisted. "Just go around the room and pick up all the stuff that we should take upstairs. Make one pile for our room and one pile for the boys' room."

"I don't see anything," Audrey whined.

"Look right under your nose," Isabel said. "That's your sweater. You took it off in here last night."

"I was hot."

"It belongs upstairs in our room. Put it in the pile."

"What pile?"

"Start a pile."

"Doesn't Frank have to help?" Audrey whined.

Isabel glanced at Frank, who seemed to be dozing. "Let's make this our special surprise," she said to Audrey. "We'll do it together."

Eddie pulled himself up on the coffee table and slapped it with the palm of his hand. In a moment, Barbara was at his side and joined in the banging.

"Can they do that?" Audrey wanted to know.

Isabel picked up a book and laid it on top of Audrey's sweater. "I don't think they can hurt anything."

"I want to play with Frank's truck. He's asleep," Audrey said.

Isabel glanced at the sleeping boy. "Can you just help me pick up this room first? Then you can play with the truck."

"Tuck," Eddie said. He stopped banging and toddled over to the truck, idle on the floor next to the sofa where Frank slept.

Isabel picked up one sock. "Where's the mate to this sock?" she asked.

"I haven't seen it," Audrey insisted.

"But it's your sock."

Audrey shrugged and straightened a stack of old magazines under the coffee table.

Barb left the table and followed her twin to the truck. Together they rolled it away from the sofa to a clear space on the floor.

Isabel streaked her finger through the dust along the top of a bookcase. "When we're done picking up, we can dust in here, too."

The crash that came next made her heart leap. She whirled around and saw what had happened.

Barb and Eddie stood in front of the wall, pointing happily. "Tuck, tuck," they said. Giggling, they picked it up together and repeated their triumphant action. The metal Coca-Cola truck was too heavy for either of them to handle alone. But together they had managed to heave it at the wall—twice. A cloud of

19

dust and a large piece of wallboard flew out from where the truck had slammed against the wall.

Isabel raced across the room and snatched the truck up before they could do it again. The twins grinned up at her as Isabel's heart sank. Still giggling, the twins started running toward the kitchen. Isabel chased after them, grabbing one toddler under each arm just as her mother appeared.

"What was that crash?" Mama wanted to know.

"Eddie and Barbie did it," Audrey was quick to explain.

"Did what?"

"Made a hole in the wall."

Now Mama saw what Audrey was talking about. She crossed the room and knelt to examine the damage. Isabel saw her shoulders sink.

"I'm sorry, Mama," Isabel said. "I was trying to surprise you by picking up some of the mess. I guess I wasn't watching what they were doing."

Frank was awake now. "Where's my truck?" he demanded.

Audrey produced it victoriously. "You weren't taking care of it, so the twins got it."

"I was sleeping!" Frank said in his own defense.

"Children, please," Mama said, "it's not anyone's fault. Stop blaming each other."

"But you asked me to watch the twins, and I didn't," Isabel said.

"Yes, you did," Mama assured her. "I know how fast they can be, especially when they're doing something together. It's not your fault."

"Can Daddy fix the wall?" Audrey asked.

"He'll have to try," Mama said. "This house belongs to Mr. Hayden. We can't go around knocking holes in the wall and not fix them."

Mama said nothing more. But Isabel knew what she was thinking. Fixing the wall was going to cost money. Daddy was already working hard just to feed and clothe the family. How would he find time or money to fix a hole in the wall?

"Mama, I have a headache," Frank said, as he slumped back on the sofa.

CHAPTER 3
Bad News

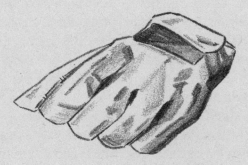

Frank's headache worsened. Then the cough began. At last the fever came. Mama tended him carefully, bathing him in cool water to keep his fever down and urging him to drink fruit juices that she could barely afford to buy. Still, he became sicker. When his chest became heavy and he labored to breathe, Mama at last called the doctor.

Dr. Reynolds came and listened carefully to Frank's chest. Isabel and Steven stood in the doorway of the boys' bedroom, careful to keep the younger children out of the way, while Mama and Daddy listened carefully to what the doctor had to say. There was an infection, he said, in Frank's lungs. He would have to be watched very carefully. If he did not get better in a few days, they should take him to the hospital.

Isabel cringed at what she heard. Frank in the hospital!

For the first few days after the doctor's visit, Frank did not seem to be any better. He was too weak even to walk downstairs. Several times a day, Mama took a tray of food up to him, but usually she brought it all back down because Frank didn't have any appetite.

Finally the day came when Frank seemed to improve. He woke up in the morning and told Steven he was hungry. Hastily, Mama fixed a plate of food and took it up to him. When he ate almost all of it, the whole family cheered. Isabel allowed herself to feel relief that Frank would get better. She did her best to help keep Audrey and the twins quiet so Frank's rest would not be disturbed and Mama would not have something else to worry about.

During the ten days after Frank fell ill—and the twins put a hole in the wall with his truck—Isabel was extra careful to look after the twins and Audrey. She raced home from school in the afternoons, checked on Frank, and played every game she could think of with Audrey and Ed and Barbara.

On nice afternoons, she took them outside to let them run around. Barb loved to be chased, and Eddie loved to be caught, scooped up, and tickled on the tummy. Isabel made herself breathless running after them. Audrey sneaked a spoon out of the kitchen and entertained herself digging in the dirt at the edge of Mama's vegetable garden.

Daddy had fixed the hole in the wall with the help of a friend who was a carpenter. Not very many people were building new houses, so Daddy's friend had plenty of time to help. They patched the wall using supplies left over from other jobs and then neatly painted over it. Still, every time Isabel looked at that spot, she could see the repair. She only hoped Mr. Hayden, who owned the house, would be pleased when he saw it.

Maybe he'll never see it, Isabel thought. *He only comes to collect the rent, and he never comes inside.* Still, she hated to look at that spot on the wall and remember what happened. From now on, she determined, Mama would be able to trust her completely.

Frank was well enough now to sit in the front room and look out the window while Isabel played with the twins. From the small front yard, she waved at his pale face in the window.

"Bel-bel down!" Barb tugged on Isabel's hand until the older sister gave in and plopped to the cold ground. Barb immediately threw herself on top of Isabel, giggling and squealing. But even while playing with Barb, Isabel never took her eyes off her little brother.

"Eddie, come back!" she called when he started to wander too close to the street. Springing to her feet despite Barbara's weight on her stomach, Isabel reached for Eddie's hand and guided him back to a safer area.

"Tees!" Eddie squealed at the sight of his oldest brother.

Steven sauntered into the yard with a baseball bat over one shoulder.

"How was your game?" Isabel asked.

"One of the best yet. That Richie Harrison has got one of the best arms in the city. He'll play pro ball someday, I'm sure of it." Steven bounded up the steps and pulled open the front door.

Isabel followed more slowly, holding one twin by each hand.

"Mama, you should have seen us play today," Steven told his mother.

Mama looked up from her ironing. "Tell me all about it, every play."

"How about just the highlights?"

"My ears are yours." She set her iron upright and crouched in front of the ironing board as if she were playing shortstop.

"It was the fifth inning," Steven began, "and we were down three runs to two. But we had the heart of the batting order coming up."

Mama pressed her lips together and looked somber. "This is serious business." She rubbed the fronts of her thighs, ready to play ball herself.

"First, Tom was up to bat. And he almost got on base. He smacked the ball pretty good."

Mama swung an imaginary bat at the empty air and raised her eyes to the horizon.

"But the fly ball was caught," Steven said.

Mama smacked one hand into the other, then returned to her crouched, ready position.

Isabel laughed. Some of her parents' friends said that Lydia Harrington was an overgrown child sometimes. Isabel did not care. She loved it when her mother went on imaginary adventures with her, just as much as Steven loved reliving his baseball games.

"So then it was Dick's turn. When he had two strikes, he finally took a swing."

Mama swung again.

"But he barely tipped the top of the ball, and it just drib-bled across the infield."

Mama snapped her fingers. "Oh, no!"

"But this is the best part. The shortstop reached down to scoop it up—and he missed! It went right between his legs."

Mama was bent at the waist, watching the imaginary ball roll between her legs and into the outfield of the kitchen.

"So Dick was on first. We couldn't believe it."

25

Isabel giggled as Mama put her hands to her cheeks and looked astounded.

The back door opened, and Alice came in.

"How was work, Alice?" Mama asked, not changing her pose.

Alice laughed. "Are you in the middle of a baseball game here?"

Mama nodded. "We need you in right field."

Alice put her purse on the kitchen table and took up her position. "What's the score?"

Mama and Isabel looked at Steven, who said, "The score is three to two. We're behind, and we have one out and one man on base."

"All right, I'm ready," Alice said, rubbing her hands together and bending her knees slightly.

"Pay, pay!" Barbara pleaded.

"Yes, you can play," Isabel said. She lifted her sister to her hip and turned toward Steven.

"Now it was my turn to bat. I knew that this was our last chance. After me comes Peyton Johnson, and he's not much of a hitter when it matters most. So I concentrated as hard as I could."

Mama licked her lips and brushed her golden bangs out of her eyes. She stared at Steven as if her life depended on it.

"So I took the bat," Steven said.

Mama picked up a bat once again and got ready to swing.

"The pitch came in high and on the outside, but I thought I could get it."

Mama raised herself to her tiptoes and stretched her arms.

"It wasn't a very good pitch, but something told me I should swing, so I did."

Mama swung.

"And I hit it! A long way!"

Mama raised her eyes to the horizon once again.

Steven started trotting around the kitchen. "The ball barely stayed fair, but it did. When it landed in the outfield, it started rolling. I had plenty of time to run. Dick scored and so did I."

"Now the score is four to three, in your favor," Isabel said.

Steven scooped up Eddie and swung him around in the air. "And that's the way it stayed. Thanks to Richie Harrison's terrific pitching, we held them there the rest of the game."

Isabel laughed. "You make it sound so much more exciting than it really is. It takes too long to watch a real game."

Mama swept her hand across her forehead in relief. "Whew! Another tense moment in the history of baseball." She spat on her iron to test the heat. The sizzling and bubbling told her the iron was ready. She put one of Daddy's shirts across the ironing board.

"Mama, do you want me to start supper while you do that?" Alice asked.

"I suppose we're having potatoes again," Steven said.

"Not on your life," Mama answered. "Noodles!"

Everyone laughed. If supper was not potatoes, then it was noodles in some form or other. Alice moved to the sink to fill a pot with water. With the snap of a match, she lit a front burner on the stove.

"Flat or curly?" Steven asked.

"Flat. And I have a surprise. In view of Steven's astounding accomplishment this afternoon, we shall each feast on one meatball tonight."

"Meatballs? Really?" Steven's eyes lit up.

Alice was suspicious. "How many cracker crumbs did you roll in with the meat?"

"That's not important." Mama pressed the hot iron down on the shirt collar.

"I don't care," Steven said. "Mama can make it taste like meat even if it's all crackers."

In Steven's arms, Eddie gurgled and his eyes brightened. "See?" Steven said. "Even little Eddie wants a meatball."

The back door opened again, and Daddy came through. He set his briefcase on the floor next to the door and greeted his family. Mama leaned over the ironing board to receive her kiss.

"How's Frank?" Daddy asked.

"Better," Mama answered. "He's been sitting up most of the day, and he ate all of his lunch."

Daddy glanced around the room. "And Audrey?"

"Outside digging," Isabel explained.

Daddy scooped up the twins from Steven and Isabel and gave them both juicy wet kisses on their soft cheeks. Barbie giggled and kissed her father in return. "I am delighted to see every one of you," he said, squeezing the babies.

"You missed Steven's baseball story," Alice said.

"I'm sure it was a good one. I'll have to hear it later. I'm a bit tired right now."

"Donald, what's wrong?" Mama asked.

"It's been a long day," he answered.

Mama was not satisfied. "Donald, if something is wrong, I want to know."

Daddy looked at all the faces in the room. "I guess everyone here is old enough to hear my news. The twins won't understand anyway."

"I knew it!" Mama said. "Something happened."

Isabel heard the alarm in her mother's voice.

Daddy reached into his pocket and handed Mama an envelope. The color drained from her face as she sat down in a chair and opened it. Even the twins were quiet, waiting to hear what it said.

Daddy turned to the children. "I've been let go," he said quietly. His dark eyes sagged.

"Let go?" Isabel echoed. "What does that mean?"

"It means Daddy has lost his job," Alice explained.

"But why?" Steven protested. "You know more about those machines at the mill than anyone else there. You designed some of them yourself."

Daddy nodded. "That's all true. But the company is just not making enough money to support the whole design group. They had to let some of us go."

"Others have lost their jobs, too?" Mama asked.

Daddy nodded somberly. "They're cutting staff in every part of the mill. Wilfred Stoner has been in the design group five years longer than I have. So they kept him. They assure me that as soon as they can afford to hire me back, they will."

"Oh, Daddy, I'm so sorry," Alice said. "I know how much you love your job."

"I have always enjoyed working at Pillsbury," Daddy said. "But it looks like God has another idea right now."

I hope God has an idea, Isabel thought, seeing the stunned expression on her mother's face. *Alice's paycheck for ten hours a week at the pharmacy is not going to support this family.*

CHAPTER 4

Midnight Plans

Isabel kicked at her covers and rubbed her eyes. She did not really want to wake up, but the bathroom was clear down at the end of the hall, and she had to wake up enough to get there without tripping over her own feet.

It felt like she had been sleeping for a long time, but she could not see the clock. If she turned on a light, she would wake up Alice or Audrey. So she threw her legs over the side of the bed and slid her feet into her waiting slippers. Then she carefully felt her way along the wall to the door.

Alice's blankets rustled as she turned over in the other side of the bed the three sisters shared. Barbara snored gently in her crib near the door. Isabel turned the knob and pulled slowly, wincing at the squeak. The hallway was just as dark. She trailed her fingers along the wall to guide her steps.

Done with the bathroom, Isabel walked back down the dark hall with one eye closed. She shivered. Even though the days were sunny, the house grew cold at night when Daddy did not put any more coal in the old furnace. Isabel closed her eyes long enough to rub them as she walked.

Suddenly she banged up against something and nearly lost her balance. She lurched against the wall with a thud.

"Ow!" she cried as she struck her funny bone on the wall.

"Shhh!"

Opening her eyes wide now, Isabel saw Steven's shadowy form huddled in the hallway. She squeezed her right elbow with her left hand and tried not to scream.

"What in the world are you doing?" she whispered.

"Shhh." Steven pointed through the stair railing at a dim light on in the front room.

"Mama and Daddy are still up?" Isabel asked. "It must not be as late as I thought it was."

"It's late, all right," Steven assured her. "They've been down there talking for hours."

"And you've been listening?"

Steven shrugged. "I didn't mean to, at first, but I got interested."

Now Isabel was interested, too. She crouched next to her brother. "What are they talking about?"

"Seattle."

"Seattle? The city in Washington?"

Steven nodded.

"What about it?"

"I'm not sure. I can't hear very well from up here."

"How long have you been trying?" Isabel asked, chiding her brother with her tone.

"I only woke up a few minutes ago. But they're down there, sitting just like they were when we went to bed."

"Mama likes to stay up late. She says it's the only time she can be alone."

"I know, but Daddy gets up so early that only something really important would make him stay up this late."

"Maybe now that he doesn't have a job, he won't get up so early."

"Oh, yes he will."

"I guess we'll have to wait until the morning to ask what this is all about," Isabel said.

Steven shook his head. "Not me. This is too important. I'm going to get closer and try to hear what they're saying."

Isabel hesitated for a moment. She knew she shouldn't eavesdrop on her parents, and she was surprised that Steven would. He was a serious person and did not do anything just for the adventure of it like Isabel did. If Steven was sure this was so important, maybe she should be, too.

Steven crept down the stairs one at a time. Isabel followed slowly. The fourth stair down always creaked, so they stepped over it carefully.

Huddled against the railing once again, they looked at each other and nodded. From where they were now, they could see straight into the front room. Daddy had kicked off his shoes and had his feet up on a footstool. Mama was in her favorite ragged bathrobe. The sofa was strewn with papers and books that had not been there earlier in the evening. Barb and Eddie would have had those papers shredded in half an instant.

Isabel could see the clock on the wall. It was nearly two in the morning.

"What is all that stuff?" Isabel asked in her lightest whisper.

"Maps," Steven answered. "I saw them on the table after supper."

"So that's why you're so curious. You knew something was going on."

"Shh!"

They sat silently and listened.

"It sounds like a wonderful opportunity for you, Donald," Mama said. "You've always wanted to design something besides flour mill machinery. This would be a perfect job for you."

Daddy nodded. "Yes, I would love to work on building airplanes. I never dreamed I would have the opportunity to do it."

Mama smiled. "Well, it seems you have the opportunity after all."

Daddy shook his head. "I'm not too sure about that. Just last year Boeing laid off hundreds of workers."

"But now they're getting contracts from the army."

"Yes, for bombing planes. I'm sure they don't want the Germans to think there are any weaknesses in the U.S. Army."

A shadow passed Mama's face. "Just because they are building bombers, we shouldn't think there's going to be another war."

"I'm sorry, Lydia," Daddy said gently. "I know how proud you are of being German. I don't for a moment believe all the lies people make up about the Germans."

"Thank you, Donald. But we're not talking about my German family. We're talking about a job for you at Boeing in Seattle."

Daddy sighed. "There will be a lot of people trying to get these jobs. A lot of people have been out of work for months or years. How can I be sure I would get a job if we moved out there?"

On the stairs, Steven and Isabel stared at each other with wide eyes. Would the family really move to Seattle? Their family had been in Minneapolis for generations. It was hard to imagine living anywhere else.

Mama picked up a map and spread it across her lap. "You have special qualifications, Donald. You're an engineer—a good one. You know how to design machinery that will work well."

Daddy smiled. "You flatter me. But the executives at Boeing might not see it that way."

"Of course they will."

"Are you so sure that we should move? It means uprooting the children and leaving our families."

"I know. Seattle is two thousand miles away. And I know Pillsbury said they would take you back as soon as they could. But that could be a very long time."

"I could do odd jobs for a while, and we could stay here."

"You would be miserable," Mama said. "Besides, who can afford to pay someone for odd jobs these days?"

"What about the children? Is it fair to them to move?"

Mama pressed her lips together thoughtfully. "Let's see. Alice is almost sixteen. She'll soon be on her own. If she decides she wants to move back to Minneapolis in a couple years, we won't stand in her way."

"And the others?" Daddy asked.

"Steven will have a lot of opportunities in Seattle," Mama said. "The university has a good athletics department—you said so yourself. He's very excited about the rowing team he's been reading about in the paper. And Isabel will think it's all a grand adventure. You know how she is, never afraid to take on a challenge."

"Just like her mother," Daddy said. "I suppose the other

children are young enough that a move won't bother them."

Mama agreed. "One of the benefits of having so many children is that they can all keep each other company while they make new friends."

"And if that doesn't work, they always have you," Daddy said with a twinkle in his eye.

Mama smiled. "I don't believe that being a grown-up means you can't have any fun."

"You're a good example to me."

"So do you think the car will take us to Seattle?"

Daddy shrugged. "It will take some work. But I don't see how else we can get there. Train tickets for nine people would cost a small fortune. We won't be able to take much with us, you know."

Mama shrugged as she looked around the room. "We can replace everything. The important thing is for the family to stay together and for you to find work that makes you happy."

Isabel nudged Steven. "Do you think they'll really move us to Seattle?"

"It sure sounds that way to me," he answered.

"We've always lived in this house, and Mama says Minneapolis is a good place to live. But I think it would be exciting to go somewhere else."

"So you wouldn't mind?"

Isabel shook her head. "Not one bit. And even if I did mind, I would do whatever Mama and Daddy thought was best for the family."

"Of course you would," Steven said. "They can't very well leave you here."

"My knees are hurting," Isabel said. She shifted her position. Her heart sank as she felt one slipper come loose and watched it thump down the stairs. She lunged after it and landed with a thud three steps below Steven. He put his fingers to his lips. Isabel scrambled back up the stairs, wishing she had just let her slipper fall.

"Did you hear something?" Mama asked, turning her head toward the stairs.

"It's probably Isabel getting up to go to the bathroom," Daddy said.

"I'll just check."

Isabel and Steven froze on the stairs. Mama's extra sharp ears heard everything. She got up off the sofa and shuffled toward the stairs. There was no chance to get away.

"What in the world are the two of you doing on the stairs in the middle of the night?" Mama asked, her arms crossed in front of her.

Steven swallowed hard. "We were curious about why you and Daddy were up in the middle of the night."

Mama glanced over her shoulder at her husband. "We had some things to talk about. It's difficult to have a conversation when all you children are around."

"Are we moving to Seattle?" Isabel blurted out.

Mama's face softened. "So you have been listening."

"I'm sorry, Mama," Steven said. "But I just knew something important was happening."

"Just how much have you heard?" Mama asked.

"Daddy might get a job at Boeing building planes to bomb the Germans," Isabel said.

"Not all of Boeing's planes are bombers," Mama said softly. "There may be other projects Daddy could work on."

"Are we really going to move?" Steven asked.

"Why don't you come in the front room, and we'll talk about it."

Isabel breathed a sigh of relief. They had been caught

eavesdropping, but Mama was not angry. They followed her into the front room, where she pushed away some of the papers on the sofa so they could sit down.

"Donald," Mama said, "we have a couple more opinions that we can consider in our decision-making process."

Daddy raised his black eyebrows. "Shouldn't you be asleep?"

"They should be," Mama said, "but they aren't. And I don't blame them. I thought we might as well begin talking about this right now."

"Daddy, if you really want to get a job at Boeing, I think we should go to Seattle," Isabel said. "It would be fun to have my father working on airplanes instead of bread dough."

Daddy laughed. "When you put it that way, it does seem quite a bit more exciting than working for Pillsbury. But it will be a risk. We can't be sure I'll get hired."

"Of course you will," Steven said.

"So you think we should go?" Daddy asked, turning to Steven.

Slowly Steven nodded. "I like living in Minneapolis. But there are lots of other places in the world I would like to see, too. Seattle can be first."

"Actually, you would see quite a bit of the United States," Daddy said. "We'll have to drive, and it will take a long time. We'll cross the northern plains states and then head into the far west."

"When will we go?" Steven asked.

Daddy and Mama looked at each other.

"Right away, I suppose," Daddy said. "We would have to get out there while Boeing is still hiring new workers."

"Can we go tomorrow?" Isabel asked.

Mama laughed. "We may need a few days to get ready."

CHAPTER 5

The Big Sale

"Steven! Help me!"

Five-year-old Audrey stood on the front porch with a wooden wagon loaded with stuffed animals, blocks, and dolls.

Steven stood in the center of the yard. Surrounding him, laid out on blankets and sheets, were the Harrington family household goods. Steven was in charge of the sale. He hoped that soon the neighbors would start coming to see if they could find a bargain on a used sweater or a big pot or a hundred other things he would try to sell. Steven turned around to look at Audrey.

"Thanks, Audrey," he said as he moved toward her. "We can put all these things over in this corner of the yard with the other toys. They should sell fast."

"I don't want to sell them!" Audrey shrieked. She snatched the handle of the wagon back from Steven. "I want you to help me put them in the car so we can take them to Washington."

Steven sighed as he looked at Audrey's load. "Mama and Daddy talked to us about this a week ago," Steven said. "We have to choose only a few very important things."

"These are my important things." Audrey stuck out her lower lip.

"I can see that. But it's too much. We can only take what we can tie to the car or fit inside."

"Everything will fit," Audrey whimpered.

Steven shook his head. "I don't think so, Audrey, not unless you plan to leave Barb and Eddie behind. Why don't you choose one toy to keep, and we'll sell the rest."

"No! I don't want to sell my toys."

Steven took Audrey by the hand and led her to a table set up in the driveway. "Look. I've put all my favorite books here. Moving to Seattle will cost a lot of money. We all have to help."

"No one will want your silly books."

"If no one buys them, I'll give them away. But I can't keep them. And you can't keep all your things, either."

"You're mean! I'm going to tell Mama!"

Audrey wheeled around and hurtled through the door into the house. She tugged the wagon in after her, banging it against the door post.

Steven sighed. Now Audrey's demands would be Mama's problem. He was sorry he had not been able to persuade his sister to follow the plan the whole family had agreed to. Mama was in the kitchen choosing her own important items.

Steven wandered over to where his father was working on the old Chrysler, assisted by Isabel.

"Is everything all right, Daddy?"

Daddy barely nodded before he stuck his head under the hood again. "Start the engine. Let me have a listen."

Steven reached into the front of the car and turned the key. The engine fired up immediately.

"Sounds good to me," Steven said.

Daddy had his head turned to one side and was leaning in close against the engine.

"I still hear something pinging."

Steven tilted his head to one side. "I don't hear it. It's probably nothing."

"I want this car in perfect shape before we start on this trip. Isabel, hand me that wrench."

Isabel slapped the wrench into her father's open palm. She leaned in beside her father. "There won't be a thing wrong with this car when we're finished with it," she said triumphantly.

"You've been working on it for days," Steven said.

"You have to be patient if you want perfection," Isabel said. Daddy handed the wrench back to her. Once again, they leaned in and listened.

"That's better," Daddy declared. He picked up a rag and wiped his greasy hands. Isabel reached for the rag, too.

"Here comes Mama," Isabel said, pointing at the driveway.

"You'd better go help her," Daddy said.

Isabel and Steven reached Mama just before the top pan in her stack tumbled to the ground. Steven caught it with one hand. Isabel reached up for some of the kitchen utensils her mother carried.

"Are we getting rid of all of this?" she asked.

Mama nodded. "I'm saving one pot, one frying pan, a spatula, and two wooden spoons."

Steven started arranging things on an empty corner of a blanket. "Did Audrey come to see you?" he asked.

"Yes, she's quite upset."

"She can't possibly take all that stuff, Mama."

"We'll have to figure something out. It's difficult for her to give away the only things she's ever known."

"But you're giving away a lot more than she is," Isabel said, looking around the yard.

Mama shrugged. "It's nothing really. Most of it is hand-me-down junk that was given to us when we got married. We haven't bought anything new in years."

"Audrey's stuff is hand-me-downs, too," Steven said. "Alice had that wagon when she was little. And her dolls are older than Alice. I guess Audrey doesn't understand that."

"Be patient with her," Mama said. "This is a big change for her."

"It's a big change for all of us," Steven said.

"I'm excited about it!" Isabel said.

Mama handed Isabel a stack of dishes. "Here, find some place to put these."

"Aren't we taking our dishes?" Isabel asked, surprised.

"Just one bowl for each of us," Mama said. "That's all we'll need until we get settled again. These dishes are chipped and scratched, but they're good enough for another family to eat off of."

Isabel knelt on the blanket and arranged the dishes as attractively as she could. Steven had the yard well organized. Clothing was strung on a line close to the house. There was not much to string up. Most of what the Harringtons wore was too worn to try to sell. But there were a lot of books. Somehow

Mama and Daddy had always managed to find money for books—nature, art, history, and science. And now the books were spread out and arranged by category on a table they could not tie to the car.

On another sheet, vases and pictures were displayed next to a silver serving tray. Isabel was sorry her mother was selling the serving tray. She could not imagine Thanksgiving and Christmas without it. It was the only valuable thing Mama had, and she had held on to it for as long as possible.

A sign on the front porch invited shoppers to enter the house and see the furniture. The neighbors across the street had already said they wanted the sofa if Mama would give them a good price. The large oak table where the family ate was worth more than anyone would want to pay for it. But Mama would take whatever she could get and quietly put the money in her skirt pocket. The beds and dressers did not match, but they were sturdy.

Isabel stood up and caught her mother's eye.

"Mama?"

"Yes, Isabel?"

"Are you sure you want to sell everything?"

Mama nodded. "Of course. If we don't get rid of it all, we can't take our grand adventure."

"I'm glad you think it's an adventure," Isabel said. "Everyone else seems a little nervous about it."

"That's understandable. It's a big change, and we don't know what we'll find when we get there."

"That's why it's an adventure," Isabel stated.

"An adventure of faith," her mother stressed. "God will give us all the chairs and dishes we need."

"I don't think Audrey believes that," Isabel said. "Here she comes again."

Audrey thumped the wagon down the three steps leading from the porch. Then she held the wagon steady and checked on her cargo.

Mama put a smile on her face. She picked up a faded stuffed bunny. "Why, Audrey, have you still got all your treasures?"

Audrey nodded, her lower lip sticking out.

"Have you thought of anything that might not be a treasure?"

Audrey shook her head. She glared at Steven. "See? Mama knows it's not junk."

"No, of course it's not junk," Mama was quick to say. "These are your very special belongings."

"So I can take them?"

Mama knelt down so she could look Audrey in the eye. "I don't want to make a promise I can't keep. But we'll try."

"Don't sell my stuff!" Audrey said to Steven. And she marched off.

"Mama, you know we can't take all that," Steven said.

"I didn't promise her we would, just that we would try. And we will."

Steven shrugged.

Isabel pointed. "Oh, look, here comes somebody."

Soon the yard was buzzing with visitors. Many were well-wishing neighbors. While the women picked over the children's clothing and household goods, the men shook Daddy's hand and wished him luck finding a job.

"How much for this vase?" Mrs. Kessler wanted to know.

"What about the push mower?" Mr. Green asked.

"How much will you take for the set of dishes?" Mrs. Dunbar asked.

Steven and Mama flitted around the yard answering questions and collecting money. Mama's skirt pocket was starting to bulge.

The twins woke up from their morning nap. Mama asked Isabel to take the twins and Audrey and Frank into the backyard where they would be out of the way of the shoppers. The middle of April had taken the edge off of winter, and with jackets on, they could play comfortably outside.

Isabel tried to keep her younger brothers and sisters all busy with Ring Around the Rosie and races and every other game she could think of. All this did not leave her much time to think about what was going on in the front yard. But whenever she could, she peeked around the side of the house to see what was still out on the blankets and sheets.

When Isabel took the younger children into the house for lunch, two women she did not recognize were standing in the kitchen examining the oak table.

"Did you see this chip over here?" one of them said. "And there's a scratch right down the middle of the leaf."

"Hardly any of the chairs match the table," the other said.

Isabel ignored them and sat the children in the mismatched chairs. This might be the last meal they ate at this table. She passed out slices of bread with butter and split one orange among all five of them.

"I think she's asking a bit much," the first woman said.

"She has to sell the table," the other answered. "You should be able to get it for practically nothing. Make her an offer."

The first woman looked sternly at Isabel. "You take care you don't scratch this table any more."

"Yes, ma'am." Isabel wanted to say a lot more. But she clamped her mouth shut for her mother's sake.

"Is that lady going to buy our table?" Audrey asked after the women had gone.

"Probably," Isabel said. "But don't worry. We'll get a beautiful new table in Seattle."

"I like this table. I like this house."

"Frank," Isabel said as she took her last bite, "look after the twins for a minute, please. I'll be right back."

While the other children ate, Isabel walked through the rooms to see what was left. Steven was standing in the upstairs hall.

"Somebody bought my bed. I guess Frank and I will sleep on the floor from now on."

"The front room is already empty," Isabel answered, "and there is a lady who wants the table and chairs."

"The walls look so bare."

"I know. Mama always liked having pictures up. I'm sure she'll find some new ones in Seattle."

"How can you be so sure that Seattle will be wonderful?"

"It's an adventure," Isabel responded. "An adventure of faith is what Mama calls it. I'm not exactly sure what she means by that."

"Faith means that you believe something even if you can't see or touch it. Mama has a lot of faith."

"I guess that's why she's so good at adventures."

CHAPTER 6

The Adventure Begins

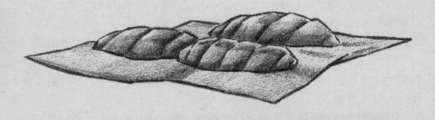

Isabel groaned as she turned over. She bumped her chin on Barbara's foot. Her thin blanket was tangled around her ankles, and her back was stiff. Sleeping on the floor had been fun at first. It reminded her of the adventure that lay ahead. But the floor was hard, and her pillow was flat. She missed the mattress she had shared with Alice and Audrey.

Even the twins had lost their cribs. Mama had stacked several towels to make a padded spot on the floor where Barbara could lie between Audrey and Isabel. Alice's spot was on the other side of Audrey.

The boys were not any better off. Everyone kept one blanket. Nine blankets, and no more, would be rolled up and

46

packed under the seats of the Chrysler. Isabel hoped that Seattle was warmer than Minneapolis.

Suddenly Isabel sat bolt upright. She was wide awake. Today was the day! The sun was shining brightly through the window. It was morning! She should not be lying on the floor complaining about not having a bed. She should be up and dressed and ready to load the car. Today was the day they would leave on their grand adventure of faith.

Isabel nudged her sisters. "Get up!" she said to Alice and Audrey. "It's time to go."

"Are Mama and Daddy up?" Alice asked sleepily. She did not open her eyes.

"They must be. I don't know how they could sleep on a morning like this."

Audrey sat up and rubbed her eyes. "Did they pack my wagon?"

"They said they would try. You'll have to go see."

Isabel was on her feet now and scrambling into her overalls. "Get dressed, Audrey. Mama has a valise for our night-clothes downstairs."

Barbara had awakened and was starting to crawl on top of Alice. She poked a pudgy finger into her oldest sister's cheek.

"Barb, you don't know what a big day this is," Isabel said. "But you're going to love it in Seattle."

Isabel scampered down the stairs to the kitchen. Mama was setting out rolls and pouring coffee.

"Are these from the bakery?" Isabel's eyes widened at the sight of the fresh bread.

"I didn't have anything left in the house," her mother explained. "So we're having bakery rolls for breakfast."

"It's a celebration!" Isabel declared. She picked up a roll and bit into it. The buttery, flaky texture melted in her mouth.

She had not tasted anything so delicious in months.

"Are we going to eat in restaurants all the way to Seattle?"

Mama shook her head. "That would be really fun—and expensive, I'm afraid. We'll buy some things for sandwiches and have picnics along the side of the road."

"Where's Daddy?"

"He's outside checking a few things on the car. You can go out and tell him his coffee is ready."

Taking her roll with her, Isabel dashed out the back door and around the house to the driveway. The early May morning was chilly but promised clear skies for traveling.

"How does she sound?" she asked eagerly.

"Purrs like a kitten," her father answered, obviously pleased.

Isabel stuffed another bite in her mouth. "I can't wait. Oh, Mama says your coffee is ready."

"I'll need plenty of that. I was up half the night getting everything tied down."

He lifted his eyes to the top of the load on the roof of the car.

Isabel followed her father's gaze. "Audrey's wagon!"

Daddy shook his head. "I can't promise her how long it will stay up there, but we'll give it a try. The rest of you will have to put up with the animals and dolls in the back."

Isabel and Daddy went back into the house. The whole family was up.

"Come here, you two," Alice was saying as Isabel pulled the back door open. Giggling, the twins scampered out of Alice's reach. She had no choice but to chase them. The table and chairs had been carted away more than a week ago, and the kitchen had become an open playground for the babies. They squealed as they ran from Alice and hid behind Frank.

Just as Alice reached them, they let go of Frank's legs and took off across the room again.

As they ran past Isabel, she grabbed Barbara. Eddie stopped to see what had happened, and Alice snatched him up. Together, the sisters set the babies on the floor in one corner of the room. Alice set some bread in front of them, but neither of them seemed interested in eating.

"They're too excited, I guess," Alice said.

Isabel grinned. "It's going to be a great day."

Mama was straightening Audrey's cotton dress. An open suitcase lay on the floor next to her.

"If you have any last minute things to pack," Mama said, "I still have one suitcase open." She turned and started refolding the assorted clothing in the valise.

"Lydia, did you have something to eat?" Daddy asked.

"Not yet. I haven't been able to stand still long enough to eat."

"You'd better have something. It will be a long day."

"Bel-bel," Barb cooed.

"Tees!" Eddie said more emphatically as he pointed at Steven.

Then the two little ones were on their feet again, their breakfast untouched.

Mama sighed. "Let's just wrap up the extra rolls and take them with us. Maybe the twins will feel like eating later." She snapped the suitcase shut.

Audrey crammed the last of her bread into her mouth and said, "I'm going to go look for my wagon."

"Don't talk with your mouth full," Mama said.

Isabel and Daddy looked at each other and smiled.

"Let's take that last suitcase out," Daddy said. Isabel picked it up and started back outside.

"Daddy, you did it, you did it!" Audrey squealed. "We're taking my wagon!"

Isabel decided to take a closer look at what Daddy had spent the night doing. Daddy and Mama's mattress, the only one they had not sold, was tied to the flat roof of the Chrysler. Four large, odd-sized suitcases, holding clothing for nine people, were laid side by side across the mattress. Mama's favorite wooden rocker was laid on its side and tied to the top of the suitcases.

The whole family knew how much Mama loved that rocker. Daddy had insisted that she not put it in the sale, and Isabel was glad. The chair was a wedding present from Mama's parents, and Mama had rocked all of her seven babies in it. She deserved to keep her favorite chair.

Assorted boxes of smaller items that family members did not want to give away were tucked in around the rocker. The whole pile was covered with a canvas tarp tied down at the corners. Then on top of the stack, as an afterthought, was Audrey's worn, wooden wagon.

"Thank you, Daddy, thank you!" Audrey screeched. She lunged into the car and started arranging her stuffed animals and dolls.

Around the back rim of the car, behind the doors, Daddy had rigged a rope to hang things from. The few pans that Mama had kept were strung on the rope, along with assorted gardening tools and a bag of dishes.

Steven came out the front door with his arms full of towels and sheets.

"We have to find places for these," he said. He crawled inside the car, followed by Isabel.

Audrey was lining up her dolls on the seats.

"Where are we supposed to sit?" Steven asked.

"You can sit on the floor," Audrey answered. She added her favorite doll to the row, the one with most of her hair missing and one eye poked out.

Steven sighed and set his stack of towels on the seat. "Audrey, we have nine people in the family. The people get to sit on the seats. The dolls have to go somewhere else."

Audrey howled in protest.

"Steven's right," Isabel said sternly. "We have to have room for the towels and sheets, and all the blankets and pillows have to fit somewhere or we'll have nothing to sleep with at night."

Pouting, Audrey snatched up her dolls and clutched them to her chest.

Steven rolled his eyes. At least the seat was clear now. He bent over and began tucking sheets and towels into the odd-shaped spaces under the seats.

"We'll have to hold the twins," Isabel said.

"We always do," Steven replied. Even with the babies on their laps, it would be hard to fit nine people in the car. For the short ride to church, they had never minded it. But a long ride across the country with boxes tucked under their feet would be a lot more uncomfortable.

"I won't mind," Isabel said. "The adventure is the important thing. So what if it's crowded for a few days?"

Alice arrived with a stack of folded blankets. "Have you got space for these? Mama is coming with the rest."

Steven thought for a moment. "We'll have to spread them out on the seats and sit on them."

"That's a good idea!" Isabel grabbed the first blanket off the pile and opened it up. "We can put some on the floor, so that the little kids will have a soft place to play."

Frank climbed in next, with his metal Coca-Cola truck

tucked under his arm. Audrey instantly lost interest in her dolls.

"Can I play with your truck?"

"No!" came the quick response.

"You two are not going to fight over that truck all the way to Seattle, are you?" Steven asked. "Maybe we should tie it to the rope on the back of the car."

"No!" Frank protested. "I promise to share."

"Everybody try to find a place to sit," Alice directed. "Some of us will have to sit on the floor. I'll go see if Mama needs help with the twins."

Mama and Daddy arrived, each carrying one baby and a bundle of pillows. They leaned in through the open door and set the twins down. Daddy walked around to the other side and got in the driver's seat, while Mama sat next to him in the front.

"Everybody in?" Daddy called over his shoulder.

Isabel looked around. Everybody was there, squeezed in shoulder to shoulder, knee to knee. The Chrysler B-70 was one of the biggest cars around, but it was still crowded for nine people. She held Barbara on her lap, while Steven had Eddie. Alice tried to help Audrey and Frank get comfortable on the floor. Audrey insisted that all her dolls had to be comfortable, as well. Finally everyone was settled.

"We're ready, Daddy," Isabel said. "Let's head for Seattle."

Daddy turned around in his seat. "Before we go, let's ask God to keep us safe on our journey."

They bowed their heads.

"Fold your hands, Barbara," Isabel said. She held her sister's tiny hands together and closed her own eyes.

"Our heavenly Father," Daddy began, "in faith we have decided to move to Seattle, and in faith we trust You to get us there safely. We pray for safe traveling, good health, and cheerful spirits. We know that You love us and want to take care of us. We place ourselves in Your hands to provide for all our needs. We ask this in Jesus' name. Amen."

Isabel's heart pounded with excitement. The grand adventure was about to begin.

Daddy held the key between his fingers and put it in the ignition. He turned it, and the engine ignited.

"Yeah!" came the chorus from the back.

Daddy put the car into reverse and slowly backed out of the driveway. The car creaked under the load on the roof. Isabel winced. They had spent a lot of time making sure the car's engine was perfect, that the radiator would not overheat, that the brakes were dependable. They had not thought about how the extra load on top would affect the car. The old car seemed to groan and howl in protest.

Now they were on the street. Daddy put the car in forward gear and pressed the accelerator. As they picked up speed, the twins burst out crying.

"What's the matter?" Daddy asked. He had to speak loudly.

"It's all the noise," Mama answered. "They're frightened of the racket."

There was indeed a racket. All the tools and pans hanging from the rope in back clanged against the car. The handle of Audrey's wagon thumped rhythmically against Mama's rocker. And the canvas tarp flapped in the wind ferociously.

Frank clambered off the floor and crawled into the seat between Steven and Isabel to look out the back of the car. "Is it going to be this noisy all the way to Seattle?" he asked.

"It's all part of the adventure," Isabel answered.

CHAPTER 7
A Setback

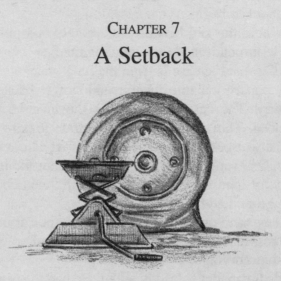

"How much longer, Daddy?" Frank asked, hoisting himself up off the floor and leaning over the front seat. He rested his chin on Daddy's shoulder.

"How much longer until what?" Daddy asked from behind the steering wheel.

"Till Seattle."

Daddy turned his head to glance at Frank. "This is only our first day, Son. We have a long way to go."

"Is it going to take a lot of days?"

"About a week, I think," Daddy said.

"A week is seven days," Audrey declared.

"That's right," Mama said.

Frank slumped back down to the floor. "A week is a long time to ride in a car. Nobody told me it would take so long to get to Seattle."

"I know it's crowded," Daddy said. "We just have to make the best of it. How is everyone else doing?"

"Eddie's finally sitting still," Steven said with relief.

Eddie was sound asleep on a pillow in Steven's lap, his bare feet buried in Alice's skirt. His mouth hung open, and his little chest rose and fell with the even breathing of deep sleep. With her head leaning against the window, Alice was dozing, too.

Isabel was too excited to think about sleeping in the middle of the day. She had never spent six hours riding in a car before. It was crowded. She ached to unbend her knees and stretch her legs straight out in front of her. Even the short stop for a picnic lunch had not taken the kinks out of her. Her toes were buried under Audrey's pile of animals, and she held two of the dolls in her lap. But she could not tear her eyes away from the window. As the countryside rushed passed, she got more excited by the minute.

"I haven't heard anything from you in a while, Isabel," Daddy said. "Are you all right?"

"I'm fine, Daddy. I can't stop looking at everything. There's so much to see." And there was. Minneapolis was a big city. You could see a lot of things without ever leaving the city limits. Isabel had heard stories about other parts of the country. Now she was going to see them for herself.

A couple years ago, Alice had made friends with Chet, a hobo who had ridden the rails of the country for months before ending up in Minneapolis. He had painted beautiful word pictures of open plains and the Rocky Mountains and high deserts. Isabel had hung on every word, hoping that someday she would see those places for herself. Now she was. She had never been out of Minneapolis before. Now she was going to spend a week crossing the country.

Steven had whooped and hollered when they crossed the border into North Dakota. Most of that state still stretched ahead of them. Even with his hands full of Ed, Steven kept his brain busy calculating the miles across North Dakota, Montana, Idaho, and Washington.

So far, Barbara had spent every minute of the car ride standing in Mama's lap. Isabel kept trying to get her baby sister to come into the back with the rest of them. Surely Mama needed a break. But even Barbara's Bel-bel could not convince her to give up her seat in the front. And Isabel did not blame her. From Mama's lap, Barbara could see everything—even before Isabel saw it. The little girl stood and stood and stood. She balanced herself in the moving car by grabbing handfuls of her mother's blond hair and keeping a firm grip. Every few minutes, Mama gently removed Barbara's sticky fingers from her hair. Unlike her twin, Barbara refused to sleep. Sooner or later she would have to sleep. Isabel did not see how a one-year-old could stand up all the way from Minneapolis to Seattle.

A sudden pop woke everyone up. Ed started to wail. The car lurched to the left.

"What was that?" Frank was clambering over the front seat again. "Did something fall off?"

Steven had twisted around in his seat to answer just that question. "I don't see anything on the road. Everything is still tied on."

"It's the tire," Daddy said. "I think we have a flat." He coasted the car to the side of the road and turned off the engine.

Daddy got out to inspect the front left tire. Steven handed the squalling Ed to Alice and climbed over Audrey and Frank to get outside also. Isabel hung her head out the window.

"It's flat all right," Daddy said.

"But we have the extra tire on the back of the car," Steven said. "We'll be fine."

Daddy sighed. "That rope with everything tied to it is strung right through the tire. And I'm not sure where the jack is. We'll have to take everything off. And the spare tire is not a very good one."

"It's all we have," Steven said sensibly. "I'll help you change it."

Daddy waved at the rest of the family. "Everybody out."

Steven dashed around and opened the doors. His brothers and sisters crawled out.

"Are we going to have lunch again?" Audrey asked.

"No, Audrey," Isabel answered. "We have a flat tire."

"A circle can't be flat," Isabel said.

"When it's a tire, it can."

Isabel followed her father until they found the end of the rope strung across the back of the car. Daddy untied the knot, and they began removing everything and setting it carefully along the side of the highway: a sauce pan, a frying pan, a big bean pot, three tools that Mama used for digging in the garden, a duffel bag of bedding supplies, an old kerosene lantern that Daddy had brought along for emergencies. At last they came to the tire. Daddy unlooped the rope and let the tire roll free.

"Isabel," Daddy said, "you're smaller than Steven. Go back in the car and crawl around the back and see if you can find the jack."

"Is that the big, black greasy thing with the long handle?"

"That's it. We can't change the tire until we find it—unless you're strong enough to lift this car." Daddy's eyes twinkled.

Isabel smiled. "I'll find the jack."

Mama spread a blanket out in the dry weeds at the side of the road. The twins climbed all over her, but she didn't seem to mind. She poked and giggled and laughed right along with them.

"Come on," Alice said to Frank and Audrey. "Let's go for a little walk." Frank and Audrey seemed glad for the chance to run freely and shot off ahead of Alice.

Back in the car, Isabel felt like she was Moses parting the Red Sea. Toys and towels and blankets and pillows all had to be moved so she could get to the back of the car and look under the seat. It was almost too dark under there to see any-thing. She reached in with one hand and waved it around. Her knuckles bumped into something cold and hard.

"Aha," she said. She ducked under the seat and came out with the tire jack.

"Good job, Isabel," Daddy said. "Let's see if we can get this tire off."

Daddy took off the sweater he had worn all day and laid it carefully on the ground next to the pots. He rolled up his shirt sleeves all the way to the elbows.

Steven was already trying to slide the jack under the frame of the car. "Start pumping," he said to Isabel.

Obediently, she started working the pump handle up and down until the jack was securely under the frame of the car. It was no small effort, but the tire was finally changed and every-thing was tied back on. Daddy squatted down to inspect the spare tire. He did not look happy.

"What's the matter, Daddy?" Isabel asked.

He stood up and patted her shoulder. "Everything's okay."

With his hands in his pockets, Daddy walked over to where Mama still sat on the blanket with the twins. She looked up at him with questions in her eyes.

"We'll have to see if we can get the tire repaired," he said quietly. "We really shouldn't drive very far on this one."

Mama stood up and brushed off her skirt. "We wouldn't be having an adventure if we knew everything that was going to happen—right, Isabel?"

Isabel looked from one parent to the other. Daddy's eyes were clouded over, but Mama's still sparkled.

"We'll have to stop for gas soon, anyway," Mama said. "We'll see what can be done about the tire then."

Daddy nodded. "Let's get going, then."

Isabel ran up the road to find Alice and Audrey and Frank. Steven made sure the rope across the back was tied tightly. The flat tire hung where the spare had been, but this time Daddy did not put the rope through it.

Everyone piled in again and settled into their assigned places. Mama tried to set Barbara in the back with Isabel, but the one-year-old protested at the top of her lungs. So Mama took her in the front again, and Barb stood on her toes as she had all day.

An hour later, they rolled into a small gas station with one gas pump. Daddy pulled the car up next to it and got out.

The attendant greeted him. "What can I do for you, sir?"

"Fill up the tank, please," Daddy answered. "Can you fix a tire?"

The attendant rubbed his greasy hands on a dirty rag. "Depends what's wrong with it."

Daddy led him around to the back of the car. Isabel hung out the window to listen. The man licked his lips while he considered the fate of the tire.

"That can't be fixed," he finally announced. "At least I couldn't guarantee that the repair would hold more than two hundred miles. But I can sell you a new tire."

Daddy nodded. "I was afraid this would be the case." Daddy and the attendant walked together away from the car and toward a display of tires.

"Isabel," Mama said. "You come up here and sit with Barbara."

Then Mama got out of the car and joined Daddy.

Frank and Audrey hung out the window. Steven sat forward on his seat.

"What are they doing?" Audrey asked.

"We have to get a new tire," Isabel answered. "Daddy has his wallet out now."

"Is he giving the man some money?" Frank answered.

"Not yet. He's talking to Mama."

They watched in silence. Even five-year-old Audrey understood that buying a new tire was going to cost a lot of money.

"I can't believe something like this happened on our first day," Alice said. "If we have a problem every day, Mama and Daddy won't have any money left by the time we get to Seattle."

"Maybe we shouldn't eat so much for supper tonight," Isabel suggested.

"What is for supper?" Frank wanted to know.

"I don't know, and it doesn't matter," Isabel answered. "The point is, we shouldn't eat very much. Food costs money, too."

"Isabel is right," Alice agreed. "We all have to make sacrifices until we get to Seattle."

The attendant took a tire off the rack and rolled it toward the garage.

"Looks like we'll have to get out again," Steven said. He reached for the door handle.

"I'm hungry," Frank said as he got out.

"Shh!" Isabel and Steven said together.

"Didn't you understand a word we said?" Isabel said sharply.

"All that talk about supper made me hungry."

"Don't talk about food where Mama can hear you." Steven's voice was firm.

"Can we go for a walk again?" Audrey asked.

"Sure," Alice answered. "Let me get my shoes on."

Audrey lined her dolls up in a perfect row before she left the car. Frank took his prized truck with him. Isabel and Steven held the twins.

Daddy walked toward them.

"This kind gentlemen is going to put a new tire on the car," he explained. "He's here by himself, so it's going to take a little while. But we'll be on our way again before long."

Mama patted her stomach. "I'm getting hungry, Donald." She turned to Isabel and Steven. "How about you two? Are you hungry?"

Isabel and Steven glanced at each other. They shook their heads.

"Lunch has been sticking to my ribs pretty well," Steven said.

"Riding in a car all day doesn't make me hungry like going to school does," Isabel finally said.

"I'll ask the attendant if he knows of a place where we can get beds and a meal," Daddy said.

Barbara squirmed in Isabel's arms. "Mama."

Mama reached out and took Barbara. "Don't look so glum, you two."

"But, Mama," Steven said. "Everything is going to cost so much."

Mama nodded. "We've had a bit of a setback. But tomorrow is another day. And God is as faithful as He always has been."

Isabel grinned. "I'm glad you're an adventurer, Mama."

Mama answered, "Faith adventures are the best kind."

CHAPTER 8
Meeting Mrs. Rogers

In the morning, Mama produced some more bakery rolls. Isabel never did figure out where they had come from. Her eyes widened and her mouth watered at the sight of them. But when Mama handed one to her, Isabel said, "I'll just have a half a roll, please."

"Are you sure?" Mama asked. "You hardly ate any supper last night."

"I'm sure." Isabel's stomach growled.

"Are you feeling all right? Perhaps riding in the car has upset your stomach."

"I'm fine, Mama, but I just want half a roll."

"Well, all right then. Perhaps you'll feel like having the rest later." Mama wrapped the leftover half roll in a dish towel and tucked it in a basket.

The night before, Daddy had found a hotel that would let all nine of them share two beds in one room. After being cramped in the car all day, the room felt spacious.

Mama had talked a grocer across from the hotel into selling her some old cheese for next to nothing. Her food basket from home included some baked beans, so the family had eaten cheese, bread, and cold beans for supper. Mama kept offering more food. But even Frank resisted the temptation to have a second helping. Mama put away enough leftover food for lunch. Somehow Mama scrounged up some milk for the babies while everyone else drank water from the bathroom tap.

The second day of driving took the Harrington family to the western edge of North Dakota. For a long time, they followed the railroad tracks. Isabel could see the long freight trains chugging across the open plains. They moved so slowly with the weight of a hundred cars or more that they seemed to be standing still at times. Their cars contained fuel and food and clothing—anything that was manufactured in one part of the United States and needed to go somewhere else.

"I wonder where Chet is," Steven said around lunchtime. "He sure was glad to get into the Civilian Conservation Corps program."

"I wonder about him, too," Isabel said. "It's hard to believe he used to wander around the country on trains."

Late in the afternoon, while Frank and Audrey dozed on the floor, Daddy said, "Keep your eyes open for a gas station. The last several we passed have been closed up."

Mama raised her eyebrows. "Are we desperate?"

"Not yet. But we will be soon."

They rode along in silence for another twenty minutes—except for Barbara's cooing and bouncing on Mama's lap. A sound sleep overnight had given her enough energy to stand for another day. She still refused to sit in the back even for a moment.

"I see one, Daddy!" Isabel said. She leaned forward and pointed down the highway. "There, with the green sign."

Daddy sighed. "Yes, it looks like it's open."

A few minutes later, they pulled into the gas station. The attendant put the nozzle into the tank, and Isabel watched the hand on the dial begin to move around. If the tank was as empty as Daddy said, it was going to cost a lot to fill it up. Steven had been keeping a secret log of how much the gasoline cost for the trip so far. He had looked over Daddy's shoulder at the hotel, so he had that amount written down. Daddy would not tell him how much the tire had cost, but Steven could make a good guess.

"Why don't we all get out and stretch our legs?" Daddy suggested. Frank and Audrey were awake by now and anxious to be out of the car.

Isabel wanted to take a walk rather than stand around the station holding Barbara.

"Come on," she said to Steven. "Let's explore."

The gas station was the first of a small string of buildings. One small brick building looked like it used to be a bank. Another was a hotel, but it had an enormous "closed" sign in the front window. At the other end of the strip was another gas station, also closed. A hardware store was still open. Four men stood outside the doors. Isabel and Steven slowed their steps.

An older man spat tobacco before he talked. "This town didn't used to be like this," he said. "Times were, folks would come in from all around to Mr. Benton's hardware. Farmers depended on him for parts to keep their machines going."

A young man shook his head. "Those were the old days, Bud. Things are changing."

"I know, I know. Nobody seems to get a good crop anymore."

"There comes a point where it ain't economical to try to farm anymore. Folks have to find jobs in the cities."

"But the cities are just as bad off," a third man said. "I moved clear down to Sioux Falls looking for work. And I'm right back here where I started, because at least my mama will put a roof over my head. A man can't find a job anywhere right now."

"The president is trying to do something about that," the older man said. "The Works Progress Administration is supposed to give people jobs and get the country moving again."

The younger man scoffed. "The WPA is only two weeks old. It's too soon to tell if it will work. Besides, the government isn't going to create jobs in a place like this."

"Let's turn around," Isabel whispered to Steven. "The tank is probably full by now."

Out of sight of the men, Steven said to Isabel, "Do you think they're right?"

"About what?"

"About finding work. What if we get all the way to Seattle and Daddy doesn't get a job at Boeing?"

"Mama would say that's part of the adventure," Isabel responded.

When they reached the gas station, Daddy was talking to the attendant. "I was hoping to find a couple days of work," he said. "I'm a good handyman. I've never run into something I couldn't fix. And I'm not too proud to work hard."

The attendant chewed on a toothpick thoughtfully. "You might try Mrs. Rogers." He pointed down the road. "She's a widow with a farm just outside of town and doesn't have a handyman. You can't miss her house. It's white with green shingles. Very well kept. I'll warn you, though, she's pretty particular."

"Thank you kindly." Daddy tipped his hat. "Come on, everybody. Let's pile in."

In front of Mrs. Rogers's house a few minutes later, Daddy parked the car and got out.

"You all stay in the car," he said. "I don't want to make a bad impression by having the twins tear up her flower bed or something." He walked confidently toward the front door.

"I thought Daddy was going to get a job in Seattle," Audrey said.

"He is," Mama answered. "We just thought a break in the drive would be nice for all of us."

Isabel and Steven looked at each other. The corner of his list of expenses stuck out of his pocket.

"Does this mean we won't have to ride in the car all day tomorrow?" Frank asked.

"That depends," Mama answered. "Let's wait and see what Daddy says."

The front door of the house opened, and an elderly woman stood in the door frame. Daddy held his hat in his hands while he talked to her. She listened carefully for a long time before giving a response. Finally Daddy turned around and walked back to the car. He got in and started the engine. Everyone leaned forward in their seats.

"Donald?" Mama asked quietly.

He turned to her and grinned. "We can stay in the barn. I've got to move the car."

"Yeah!" A cheer went up in the back seat.

"What did she say, Donald?" Mama wanted to know more details.

"She has some fencing that needs to be fixed, and her washing machine has been giving her trouble. The wringer doesn't seem to be working properly. She said a few other things might come to mind and that she could keep me busy for two days, maybe three."

"And?"

Daddy nodded. "She can pay me a little, and she said she would feed all of us."

Mama's eyes grew wide. "Donald, did you tell this poor woman that you have seven children?"

"Yes, ma'am, I did. She didn't bat an eye. She assured me they will be well fed as long as I am working for her."

Mama fell back against her seat. "God is faithful once again."

"We'll have to share the barn with a cow," Daddy said. "And the children will have to be very careful about her flower beds."

"We will, we will," Audrey and Frank promised.

"A cow?" Steven asked.

"It's the only animal she has left," Daddy explained. "And it gives more milk than she can drink. We can have as much of it as we want. She makes her own cheese. We can take some with us when we go."

Mama turned around and smiled at Isabel. "Didn't I tell you that faith adventures are the best kind?"

Daddy parked the car in front of the barn and then returned to the house, leaving the rest of the family to examine the barn. Isabel had never been inside a barn before. She could hardly wait to get inside. Frank and Audrey were right behind her as she pulled on the big red door.

The barn was not big, but they could see where other animals had once lived. Four empty stalls surrounded the one stall where a cow stood, and at the far end of the barn was the tangled wire mesh left over from a chicken coop. A large open area in the middle was where they could sleep and eat.

Frank wrinkled his nose. "It smells like the zoo in here."

Mama laughed. "Get used to it. This is home for a couple of days."

"Where are the beds?" Audrey asked.

"Wherever we put them," Mama answered. She stooped down and gathered up an armful of hay. "How big would you like your bed to be?"

Audrey's mouth dropped open. "A bed of hay?"

"Just like baby Jesus," Mama said.

"Is there a manger?" Frank asked. And he went running off to look in the stalls.

Audrey approached the stall where the cow stood swishing her tail. She stopped about ten feet away and stared. The cow stared back.

"Is that cow going to be here all night?" Audrey asked.

"Yes, she is," Mama answered cheerfully. She started piling hay in one spot for a nice soft bed.

"She makes me nervous," Audrey said.

"Oh, don't worry about an old cow," Mama said. "I'm sure Mrs. Rogers has a good latch on that stall."

"I never saw a cow this close before."

"But you've seen cats and dogs and rabbits and squirrels and lots of other animals," Mama said. "A cow is just another of God's wonderful creatures."

"Are people supposed to sleep with cows?"

Mama did not get to answer that question. Just as she opened her mouth, she saw that the twins were tearing apart the hay she had already gathered. Barbara lost her balance and plopped down on her bottom. She sank down until the hay was nearly up to her neck. Ed found that very funny and laughed so hard that he fell down, too. Then his laughter turned to howling.

"Isabel, Steven," Mama said quickly, "get the babies out of the hay. They may get hives."

Isabel and Steven snatched the twins up.

"I'll get some bedding from the car," Alice said.

"In the meantime," Mama said, "take the twins outside."

Outside the barn, Steven and Isabel set the twins down—with a warning to stay out of the flowers. The little ones toddled around the yard and the dirt driveway while Steven and Isabel followed, watching them carefully.

"We've come a long way from Minneapolis," Steven commented. "Did you ever imagine that we'd be staying on a farm?"

"It's so exciting!" Isabel glowed. "Do you think we could learn to milk the cow while we're here?"

"Do you really want to?"

"Yes, don't you?"

Steven shrugged. "I hadn't thought about it. I suppose it would be interesting."

"If Mrs. Rogers doesn't have a regular handyman, she must do it herself," Isabel said. "I'm going to be ever so quiet when she comes to do it and watch very carefully."

"Isabel," Steven said with a warning in his voice. "If you're thinking about trying to milk that cow yourself—"

"I promise I won't do that," Isabel said. "But if she should offer to teach me, I wouldn't say no."

"Well, I suppose that would be all right. But I hope we can get back on the road before too long."

"Going to Seattle is a grand adventure," Isabel said, "but milking a cow would be an adventure, too." She looked back toward the barn, wondering what time the cow would be milked.

CHAPTER 9

Attacked by Grasshoppers

Barb and Ed were finally asleep on beds of hay in the barn for their afternoon naps. Even Audrey and Frank were resting. Alice and Mama were arranging beds for the rest of the family. Steven thought he and Isabel should help, but Mama saw the excitement in Isabel's eyes and sent them off exploring.

Behind the barn stretched a wide-open field. But it wasn't much of a field, because the ground was too dried and caked for anything to grow in it. Rather than the black earth of rich farm soil, the ground was grayish and dusty. Ragged cracks remained where the ground had split open and begged for rain.

"It's like a big puzzle," Isabel said, "chunks of ground that fit together just right."

Steven nodded. "Even a city boy can see that nothing has grown here in a long time."

"I wonder how long it's been since Mrs. Rogers had a crop."

"I'd say it's been at least three years. I don't see how anything could grow here."

Out of the cracks in the thirsty earth came scraggly dry wisps of grass. They looked more brown than green and crunched when Isabel or Steven stepped on one.

"I wonder what the cow eats," Isabel said.

"You wonder about an awful lot of things," Steven commented. "But you're right. Did you take a look at that cow in the stall? She's pretty skinny."

"Look, there's Daddy!" Isabel sprinted across the hard dirt toward her father. Steven, with his long strides, was right at her heels. Behind them a cloud of dust rose from their footsteps. Breathless, they thundered to a stop and leaned against the split-rail fence.

"Is this the fence that needs mending?" Isabel asked. She hoisted a loose railing and held it where it seemed it should go.

"This is it," Daddy said.

"Why does Mrs. Rogers need a fence here?"

Daddy shrugged. "It used to keep the animals in—she had quite a few cows. But now I don't suppose she really needs it. She said it's been broken a long time."

"Then why are you fixing it?" Isabel asked.

Steven knocked her with his elbow. "Because Mrs. Rogers asked him to. It's his job."

"I hate it in school when the teacher gives us work that doesn't really need to be done."

"It's not the same thing," Steven said. "Right, Daddy?"

Daddy placed a nail and tapped it to get it started. "Well, I can see Isabel's point. But your teacher doesn't reward your efforts with a hot supper. I'm grateful for Mrs. Rogers's generosity, and I'll do whatever she asks me to do."

"Can I help?" Isabel said eagerly.

Daddy gave her the hammer and pointed at the nail he had just started. "Don't swing it too hard."

Isabel took the hammer in two hands and aimed. She hit the nail with a solid thwack on the first try. Three more hits drove it deep into the dry wood.

"That's not so hard," Isabel declared.

"I thank you for your help, but I'm sure you have some exploring to do." Daddy gazed off beyond the fence. "Most of the land you can see from here belongs to Mrs. Rogers. Be careful to stay out of trouble."

"Don't worry," Steven said, almost insulted that his father would think a thirteen-year-old would get into trouble.

The land was flat as far as they could see. What had once been a grassy field for the cows to graze in became an open wheat field—without the wheat. When the wind stirred, the dry soil swirled in the air. There was no moisture in the ground to hold it down. Isabel and Steven could see the rows plowed in the ground for the last planting. Straight, endless lines told them that this farm had once had an abundant harvest of wheat.

"I wonder if the Pillsbury mill in Minneapolis ever got any wheat from North Dakota," Isabel mused.

Steven smiled. "There you go, wondering again."

"I can't help it. Do you suppose they did?"

Steven shrugged. "I never thought about it before. Daddy designed machines, and the machines made flour. I never thought much about what happened before or after."

"They had to get the wheat from somewhere to make the flour," Isabel said. "They could have gotten it from Mrs. Rogers."

"It's possible," Steven agreed. "And maybe she even bought some Pillsbury flour after it was shipped back out here."

Isabel looked around at the withered field. "But there's nothing here now. I don't see how those trees can stay alive much longer."

They had reached a grove of elm trees that ran along the edge of the Rogers farm. Isabel plopped down flat on her back, grateful for the shade.

"I wish we had brought some water," she said.

Steven sat beside her in the dirt. He tilted his head to one side. "Do you hear something funny?"

Isabel sat up. "As a matter of fact, I do. What is that?"

"I've never heard a noise like that before." Steven swatted at a grasshopper. "It's like…like some sort of machine. Only there's no engine, just a whirring sound."

"There sure are a lot of bugs around here," Isabel said. She slapped a grasshopper off her knee.

"It sounds more like a broken machine," Steven continued, "like something is clattering inside."

Isabel swatted a bug at the back of her neck. "We never had so many bugs in the city, especially grasshoppers."

Steven looked at her with his eyes wide open. "It's the grasshoppers," he said. "That's where the noise is coming from."

"Grasshoppers can't make this much noise." Isabel could hardly hear herself talk. She twisted her neck to look around. The noise seemed to be coming from all around them.

"If there were enough grasshoppers, they could."

73

They sprang to their feet. Suddenly the grasshoppers were everywhere, hundreds of them, thousands of them. They swarmed through the air.

"Steven!" Isabel called as she shook the bib of her overalls. A grasshopper went down the front of her shirt. "Steven!" She hopped around and slapped at her baggy pant legs until she felt the bug come out.

"We've got to get out from under the trees," Steven said. He grabbed Isabel's hand and yanked her after him. All their after-school racing had trained them to sprint, which is exactly what they did now.

Even in the field, the insects swarmed around them. Steven and Isabel paused long enough to turn around and see what they had walked into. The leaves of the trees were shaking but not from wind. And the black cloud that they had thought was dirt was moving rapidly—and noisily—after them.

"There must be millions of them," Isabel said in awe. "Millions and millions of grasshoppers."

"I'd really feel better if we were inside the barn," Steven said, and he turned to sprint across the field. Isabel followed, half-startled and half-fascinated. For a change, she did not care about winning the race.

When they reached Daddy and the broken fence, they found him with his hat over his face and the hammer lying idle on the ground. He waved them toward the barn. Steven never stopped running.

"I'll have to do this later," Daddy shouted over the din of the insects. He ran with them toward the barn and pulled the heavy door open. Isabel and Steven tumbled in just before Daddy slammed the door shut again.

Mama and Audrey and Frank and Alice had their faces pressed against the windows.

"I've never seen such a thing in all my life," Mama said. "Donald, are you all right?"

Daddy waved his arms. Three grasshoppers blew out of his shirt sleeves.

"Daddy, don't," Audrey pleaded.

Frank sneezed.

"What's the matter with him?" Daddy asked. "Is he getting an infection again?"

"Allergic to the hay, apparently," Mama said. "But he's quite fascinated by the bugs."

Mrs. Rogers popped her head up out of the cow's stall.

"So you've had an encounter with the grasshoppers," she said.

"I hope it's all right if I wait a bit before getting back to work on the fence," Daddy said.

Mrs. Rogers sighed. "They may let up after a while, but they'll be back tomorrow."

Isabel's brown eyes were wide with excitement. She walked toward the cow stall. "I didn't think there were so many bugs in the whole country, much less all on your farm."

"Oh, the other farms have their share, too," Mrs. Rogers assured her. "As if the drought were not enough of a problem, the bugs eat everything in sight."

A gasp escaped from Audrey. "Do they eat little children?"

Mrs. Rogers smiled. Mama scooped up Audrey.

"You're perfectly safe," Mrs. Rogers said. "But if I had any crops to begin with, they would be gone before the week is out. And I wouldn't be the only one." She shook her head sadly. "I never thought I'd think that the drought was a blessing in disguise. At least I didn't have my hopes up for a crop this year."

Alice was at the window of the barn, looking out at the

black cloud rumbling past them. "I've read about these infestations," she said. "They can wipe out a farm in a matter of days."

"Exactly," Mrs. Rogers said. "Unfortunately I've lived long enough to see that happen more than once. The grasshoppers, the locusts, the cicadas—they're all the same when it comes to chewing through a crop."

"And in the southern plains," Alice continued, "the dust storms blow away the soil. The air turns black, and it's hard to breathe. There's no dirt left for the plants to grow in."

"So the farmers go out of business," Daddy said.

"And food prices in the cities go up," Mama said. "Everybody loses when the farmers lose."

Mrs. Rogers nodded with appreciation. "I see you have a good understanding of agricultural economics. A farm might survive one bad year, but two or three in a row makes people give up and move to the city."

"But you haven't moved to the city," Isabel said.

Mrs. Rogers shook her head. "No, I'm too old to start over again in the city. Besides, I love this land too much. I intend to be buried under the maple tree with my husband, Henry."

"Not for a long time, I hope," Alice said.

"Mr. Harrington, your children are very sweet," Mrs. Rogers said. "I'm just an old milkmaid."

Isabel leaned on the top of the gate and peered into the stall. "Are you going to milk the cow now?"

"If I don't, Molly is likely to become very irritable." Mrs. Rogers pulled a stool off a hook on the wall and sat on it alongside the cow.

"Can I watch?" Isabel asked.

Mrs. Rogers looked her over. "You won't frighten Molly, will you?"

Isabel shook her head. "No, I promise. You tell me what to do, and I'll do exactly that."

"Do you know what an udder is?" Mrs. Rogers asked.

Isabel screwed up her face. "I read about that once in school. I've never actually seen one."

"Well, come in here, child. You're about to milk your first cow."

CHAPTER 10
Almost There

"This is like that gas station we saw in North Dakota!" Frank exclaimed. He pointed. His blue eyes gleamed in the bright sunlight. "See, the big green sign is the same."

Steven squinted into the sunlight at the sign on the corner. The oversized green letters jumped out from a dirty white background to announce the gas station. Below it was a smaller sign with that day's prices.

"I believe you're right," Steven agreed.

"Of course I'm right." Frank sounded as if he could never be wrong. "Mama always says I notice everything."

"She's right." Isabel joined the conversation. "We've seen so many gas stations. I don't understand how you boys can tell them apart."

"But they're not the same," Steven said. "Even the ones that belong to the same oil company are all a little bit different— different sizes, different kinds of pumps."

They were leaning side by side against the hood of the old gray Chrysler. The sun-soaked gray metal warmed their backs as they waited for the rest of the family to return to the car and resume their journey.

"Two thousand miles is a long way," Isabel said as she hoisted herself up to sit on the hood. She stretched her legs out in front of her. "We're far away from Minneapolis."

"I've looked at the map of the United States hundreds of times," Steven remarked. "But traveling two thousand miles across four states has taught me more geography than I ever learned at school."

"Mrs. Dixon would be really proud of you. She never thought you were going to learn any proper geography." Isabel laughed. "And I've learned a lot about dairy cows. Who would have thought that I would learn to milk a cow on this trip?"

"Are we going to have a cow in Seattle?" Frank wanted to know. He climbed up to sit next to Isabel.

Isabel chuckled again. "I don't think I learned to milk a cow well enough to have one."

"You could practice," Frank insisted.

"I don't think the cow would like that."

"Besides," Steven added, "Mama says we're probably going to live in an apartment. Cows will not be allowed."

"I think it would be fun to live on a farm," Frank said. "Don't they have farms in Washington?"

Steven waved one arm in a wide circle. "Look around.

You're already in Washington. I've seen some fruit farms along the highway."

"No cows?"

"No cows."

"Nuts. Isabel won't be able to teach me how to milk one."

Steven laughed. "Did you forget that you have problems breathing in the hay? You'll be able to learn a lot of other things. Maybe someday you'll help build an airplane, like Daddy."

"I'd like to build an airplane someday," Isabel announced. She raised her knees and tucked them under her chin. "In fact, I'm going to learn to fly one."

"But you're a girl!" Frank protested.

Isabel turned and glared at Frank. "Haven't you ever heard of Amelia Earhart? Or Jacqueline Cochran Odlum? Who says a girl can't fly a plane?"

"Well, you can't fly one in the army."

"Who says I want to be in the army? And if I did, I'd find a way."

Steven laughed. "Don't try to argue with her about that one, Frank."

"Okay, I give up," Frank said. "But what if Daddy doesn't get a job at Boeing?"

"Oh, he'll get one," Isabel said confidently.

"How can you be so sure?" Steven asked. He turned around to look at her.

"It's part of the faith adventure," Isabel answered. "Mama is sure, too."

Isabel looked over her shoulder at Mama standing in front of the gas station. The twins were gleefully pounding their open palms against the plate glass window, while Mama looked on with amusement. Audrey, nearby, straightened her doll's dress and then her own.

"Steven," Isabel said, "are you going to miss Minneapolis?"

He tilted his head to one side thoughtfully. "Maybe a little bit. After all, I've never lived anywhere else. What about you?"

"Maybe someday I'll go back to visit. But I can't wait to get to Seattle."

Daddy came out of the gas station. He had just paid for the new tank of gas and still had his wallet in his hand. He stood next to Mama and spoke quietly for a moment. Mama nodded somberly at Daddy's words, then took the twins by their hands and started to lead them toward the car. Daddy tucked his wallet back in his pocket.

"What do you think Daddy said?" Isabel said quietly to Steven.

Steven shook his head. "I think he's getting worried about money again."

"But he worked for Mrs. Rogers for four days. I thought she paid him enough to get us to Seattle."

"That's what Daddy thought, but maybe he was wrong about how much everything would cost. That hotel in Idaho was expensive, I'm sure. But it was the only place around when we needed to stop."

"Do you still have your list of expenses?"

Steven nodded and reached into his pocket. He unfolded two crumpled sheets of paper. With a stub of a pencil, he underlined the last number he had written down. "I've gone onto a second page. I added it up last night after Mama and Daddy were asleep. It's a big number." Isabel looked at it, and her jaw dropped down.

"What should we do?"

Steven shrugged. "There isn't much we can do. Just try not to complain about anything." He glared at Frank.

"Why are you staring at me?" Frank said. "I haven't said

anything about being hungry since we left Mrs. Rogers's farm."

"That's because you ate like a pig the whole time we were there," Isabel said. She pushed herself off the hood of the car. "This is getting hot. I didn't know Washington would be this hot."

"I hope there's water in Seattle," Frank said, "because I'm going to miss the river in Minnesota."

Steven laughed. "There's water everywhere around Seattle. The university has a championship rowing team, remember?"

"I learned in school that Seattle is on the Puget Sound," Isabel said.

"How can a city be on a noise?" Frank asked skeptically. He hopped down off the hot hood.

Isabel and Steven grinned. "Not the noise kind of sound," Steven explained, "the water kind of sound."

"What's that?"

"It's a stretch of water that connects two bigger bodies of water, like parts of the ocean. The whole city of Seattle is built along the waterfront."

Frank nodded. "That sounds nice, just so long as there is water."

Daddy and Mama reached them with the twins and Audrey in tow.

"Where's Alice?" Daddy asked.

"Here she comes," Audrey said, pointing at her older sister coming around the corner of the building.

"Looks like we're ready to go then," Daddy said. He pulled open the back door. "Pile in!"

In their ten days of traveling, the Harrington children had learned how to assemble themselves in the car with no wasted motion. First Alice got in. Then Steven handed little Ed to her.

She settled the toddler on her lap and squeezed herself up against the window. Next Steven and Isabel squeezed onto the seat alongside Alice and Ed. As she got settled, Isabel leaned forward and straightened the blankets on the floor. Frank and Audrey got in, and Audrey arranged her dolls and animals around her. Now Isabel's feet were trapped. She would have to sit in the same position until the next stop.

Satisfied that the passengers in the back were comfortably settled, Mama and Daddy got in the front with Barbara. For the first few days of the trip, Mama had tried to get Barbara to play in the back at least part of the time. But Barbie had a wailing will of her own, and she clearly wanted to ride in the front seat. Through four states, ten days, and two thousand miles, she had stood on her mother's lap, pointing at everything they passed.

"Wa-ney!" she squealed enthusiastically whenever they saw water.

At first Isabel was insulted that Barbara did not want to be in back with Bel-bel, as the little girl called her sister. In Minneapolis, Barbara had never turned down a chance to be with Isabel. But it was crowded in the back of the car. With all of Audrey's things scattered around the car, where would Barbara sit?

The Harringtons had left the Rogers farm three days earlier. Two days on the farm had stretched into four. Frank had to stay out of the barn away from the hay as much as possible to keep from sneezing and wheezing. So Isabel and Steven had taken him with them as they explored every inch of the place, despite the grasshoppers. They tried to imagine what the farm must have been like before the years of drought and economic depression. By the time they left, Daddy had fixed every loose latch or broken board they could find.

After they left Mrs. Rogers in North Dakota, every mile took the Harringtons closer to Seattle. Excitement built with every turn of the wheels. The Chrysler rumbled along the highway as it had all along, but the children in the back seat no longer noticed the bumps and jolts or the clanging pots hanging from the back. They were too busy absorbing the beauty of their new home state, Washington!

"Daddy?" Audrey said from her blanket on the floor.

"Yes?"

"Are we really going to be in Seattle today?"

"Absolutely, positively," Daddy answered. "In about five hours." He turned the key in the ignition and the engine purred.

"She sounds just as perfect as the day we tuned her up," Isabel said.

"That she does," Daddy agreed. He eased the car out of the gas station lot and onto the highway.

"What will our new house be like?" Audrey asked. She lined up three dolls in a neat row along the back door. "Will there be room for my babies?"

Daddy glanced at Mama, but she did not hesitate to answer the question. "There will always be room for your babies," Mama said brightly, "but they will have to share a room with your sisters, just like in Minneapolis."

"I thought maybe we would have a big new house," Audrey said.

"Maybe someday we will," Mama said hopefully. "We'll start with a smaller one."

"Will we be by the water?" Frank asked. "I want to be by the water."

"Maybe. I don't know. That's one of the surprises that are still ahead of us. I'm sure wherever we live, it will be a delightful place. We'll fix it up just the way we like it."

"I guess surprises are all right," Frank said. He pulled his truck out from under the seat and began spinning the wheels.

"Can I help you decorate the house?" Audrey asked.

"Certainly! We'll do it together."

"Can I have a blue room?"

"Perhaps, if it's all right with the landlord. Why don't we choose colors after we get there?"

"Okay." Audrey picked up a doll and began brushing its hair.

Isabel watched her father's face. He had stopped answering any questions and seemed a little nervous about what Mama was saying. *Don't worry, Daddy,* Isabel said in her head. *God will give you a job, and Mama and Audrey will be able to decorate.*

Glancing at Alice, Isabel saw that Ed was already asleep in her lap. While Barbara bounced around in the front seat, Eddie was quiet and cooperative in the back. They had been that way for the whole trip. Even twins could have very different personalities, Isabel reminded herself.

The car grew quiet as the engine hummed and the tires whirred. Isabel leaned her head against the glass and looked out at the open spaces they passed. Life in Seattle would be good, she was sure of it. Daddy would get a job, and they would find a place to live. They would see all the places they had read about before they started the trip. The grand adventure would become true life.

CHAPTER 11

Life at the Fairfax

Isabel huffed with every breath. Steven was at her heels, pounding the pavement right behind her. The only reason she was ahead of him was because she had sprinted at the very moment that she'd challenged him to a race.

"I'm catching up!" Steven declared.

Isabel was too breathless to respond. Running on the streets of Seattle meant running up and down steeper hills than she had seen in Minneapolis. The flat plains of eastern Washington were a far different territory than hilly Seattle. Steven had educated her about the Puget Sound and the waterfront they should expect to see, but he had never said a word about hills. And there were plenty of them: Queen Anne Hill, Capitol Hill, and others that did not have well-known names.

Isabel could no longer ignore the pain in her left side. She clasped her stomach with one hand and slowed her steps ever so slightly. Steven surged ahead of her triumphantly, thundered up the steps, and collapsed on the cement stoop in front of the Fairfax Hotel. Isabel threw herself down beside him and gasped for air. Their shoulders heaved with the effort of breathing, but they grinned at each other.

"You thought you had me, didn't you?" Steven gloated.

"I almost did," Isabel retorted. She leaned back on her elbows and lifted her face to the sun. "It's beautiful here. There's so much to look at. Something is happening all the time."

Steven looked up and down the street. Rows of brick apartment and hotel buildings interspersed with shops and restaurants made for a colorful neighborhood. Laundry lines strung between the buildings displayed odd sizes of well-worn clothing. The day was a warm one. Several of the neighbors were sitting out on the steps in front of their buildings. Three little girls hopscotched their way down the sidewalk, while a couple boys played catch with a baseball. At the corner, an elderly Japanese woman was doing her best to make peonies grow in a large gray pot.

"Hello, Mr. Wakamutsu," Steven said as he pulled himself to his feet. "How are you today?"

"I am fine," Mr. Wakamutsu answered formally. He began sweeping the sidewalk in front of the Fairfax with a ragged push broom. "How are you?"

"I'm fine, too," Steven answered.

"It is a beautiful day."

"I love days like this," Isabel chimed in. "The sun on my face, the breeze in my hair."

"Beautiful hair," Mr. Wakamutsu said.

"Thank you. And I love living in your hotel, too. It is also beautiful."

Mr. Wakamutsu beamed with pride. The seven-story brick building had a hotel section and an apartment section. Mr. Wakamutsu and his family looked after every detail. With the help of a few Japanese day maids, they cleaned the hotel rooms, kept the plumbing working, swept the lobby twice a day, and tended to whatever else needed to be done. One of them was always at the front desk to welcome new guests and keep the account books in order.

When the Harrington family had arrived in Seattle, they'd checked into the Wakamutsus' hotel because it was close to Boeing on the southern end of the city. If they stayed there for a few days, at the foot of Capitol Hill, Daddy would be able to apply for a job at Boeing and go back and forth very easily.

After only four days, Daddy had come home from an interview at Boeing with the good news that he would be helping to design a new bomber plane for the United States Army. The location of the Fairfax suited the whole family. No one wanted to look for another place to live. The family eagerly moved from the hotel side to the apartment side. Isabel was especially glad, because she had already started to be friends with Yoshiko, Mr. Wakamutsu's daughter. Yoshiko's two younger brothers, Kaneko and Abiko, played with Frank and Audrey.

"Is Yoshiko home?" Isabel asked Mr. Wakamutsu as he swept the sidewalk.

"She will be home soon," he answered.

"Please tell her I'm going to come down and see her in a little while."

"I will tell her." Mr. Wakamutsu bowed slightly and continued sweeping the steps.

"We'd better let Mama know we're back," Steven said. He

grinned. "Can you breathe well enough to go up the stairs?"

Isabel sighed. "So long as we don't race."

"You've got a deal."

The Harrington apartment was on the fourth floor, and there were no elevators. Breathing more easily now, Isabel pushed open the front door to the building. They started up the steps.

Inside the fourth-floor apartment, Ed and Barbara each sat wrapped around one of Mama's ankles. They giggled as she lumbered with the heavy weights on her feet. Mama looked over her shoulder when she saw Steven and Isabel come in.

"There you are! As you can see, I need to be rescued if I'm going to be able to fix supper." She turned around and lumbered toward them. The twins squealed with delight. Isabel and Steven swooped across the room and scooped up the little ones.

"Freedom at last," Mama exclaimed. "Quick! To the kitchen!"

Going to the kitchen was not much of a trip. The apartment was small, just two bedrooms, a living room, and a spacious kitchen in the back. Steven and Isabel followed Mama with the twins into the room that the family liked best.

"What's for supper?" Steven asked as he set Eddie down on the floor.

"Rice and some vegetables Mrs. Wakamutsu gave me," Mama answered.

"The rice that the Wakamutsus make is delicious," Isabel said. "Can you make it like that?"

Mama smiled. "They have a special Japanese rice steamer. I'm afraid I have to do it the old-fashioned American way."

"You're not putting any raw fish in it, are you?" Steven asked suspiciously.

"Only the eyeballs," Mama responded.

Steven let his shoulders slump and sighed. "Why do you say such outrageous things, Mama?"

Barbara squirmed in Isabel's arms. "Bel-bel." The baby swatted at her sister's face.

Isabel pulled her head back. "Do you want down?"

"Down," Barb agreed. Once down, she quickly moved to a cabinet where she knew she would find a pan. Eddie toddled over to join her. Mama had not replaced all of the kitchen equipment she had left in Minneapolis. But she had managed to gather enough items to run an efficient kitchen while still entertaining the twins.

"Did we get a newspaper yet?" Steven asked hopefully.

"Are you expecting one?" Mama asked. "You know we don't have a subscription to have one delivered."

Steven smiled sheepishly. "But some of the neighbors do. Sometimes Daddy or Alice bring home one that someone else has already looked at."

"Then you still have hope. They're not home yet."

"I want to find out how the Indians are doing," Steven said. As soon as he'd arrived in Seattle, he had begun to follow the progress of the local baseball team. "I hope that I can go see Civic Field pretty soon."

Mama filled a pot with water. "I'm sure you'll get to it before too much longer. Look at all the things you've already seen, and it's only been a week."

"That's because the public transportation is so good around here," Steven said. "All you have to do is go out in the street and hop on a trolley car and you can get anywhere you want to go."

"I enjoyed the day we all went to see the harbor," Mama said. "The boats were beautiful, all lined up along the piers."

"Boat," Barbara said.

"Yes, that's right!" Mama responded enthusiastically. "Barbara saw the boats."

"The sailboats were my favorite," Isabel said, "but most of all I liked Pikes Market. I can't believe all the vegetables for sale down there."

Steven chuckled. "The farmers come from all over the area to sell their fruits and vegetables there. Maybe Frank could be a farmer after all if he doesn't have to keep hay."

Barb had found her pan and began thumping it with her hand.

"Are we ever going to try some of the salmon for sale at the market?" Isabel asked. "I wonder what the eyeballs taste like."

Steven groaned. "You're not really supposed to eat the eyeballs. The man who sells the fish will cut off the head and tails first."

"Yoshiko says some people eat the eyeballs," Isabel said. "And they make fish tail soup. They don't want to waste any part of the fish. She doesn't really like them. There are lots of things her parents like that Yoshiko doesn't."

"You know," Steven said as he stopped Eddie from taking another pan from the cabinet, "I don't even think of Yoshiko as Japanese."

"I know what you mean," Isabel agreed. "She looks Japanese, but she was born right here in Seattle. She has never even been to Japan."

"She speaks like one of us, even though her parents' speech is so much more formal," Steven added, "and she likes all the same things that American kids like."

Mama dumped the rice into the boiling water, adjusted the lid on the pot, and turned the heat down. "That's because

91

Yoshiko is American," Mama said, "just like I am."

"Of course you're American, Mama," Isabel said. "What else would you be?"

"German," Steven answered.

"Oh," Isabel said, "I didn't think of that."

"It's because Grandpa is German, right?" Steven said.

"That's the way some people look at it," Mama explained. "When I was your age, people made fun of my German father because he enjoyed spending time with other German immigrants and liked unusual food."

"Like Wiener schnitzel?"

"Exactly. But I have never been to Germany. My father came from Germany, but I am an American, just like Yoshiko is."

Isabel looked thoughtful. "I see what you mean. Do you think Yoshiko's parents will ever become more American?"

"Do you think they need to be more American?" Mama answered with a question.

"I guess it doesn't matter, as long as they are happy."

"That's what I think, too."

Isabel laughed. "I don't want to eat the eyeballs, but I do want to try the salmon."

"Someday we will," Mama assured her, "after Daddy has been working a little longer."

"Will we ever get to go see Boeing?" Isabel asked. "I'd like to find out about how those planes are built.

"Are you moving from cars to planes?"

"If my father is going to work for Boeing, of course I'll be interested in planes." Isabel sat with her elbows on the table and her chin in her hands. "Can you imagine if we had been able to come from Minneapolis in a plane instead of a car?" Isabel said. "We could have been here in one day."

Mama looked at Barb, still thumping on the bottom of a

frying pan. "But then Barb could not have pointed at everything in the country." Mama picked up a basket of vegetables from the counter and sat down at the table to chop them.

The apartment door squeaked open. "Mama?" Alice called.

"In here," Mama answered.

Alice beamed in the doorway. "I got a job!"

Mama looked up brightly. "A job?"

"Yes! There is a family on the next block that needs someone to look after their small children for the summer. I can work three days a week for all of June, July, and August."

"I wasn't expecting you to get a job," Mama said, although she was obviously proud.

"I had a job in Minneapolis. Why shouldn't I have one here?"

"Why not, indeed?" Mama agreed. "Congratulations. Isabel, supper will be ready soon. Why don't you go find Frank and Audrey outside. As soon as Daddy gets home, we can hear all about Alice's new job."

CHAPTER 12

The Kidnapping

"Isabel!" Frank leaned out the apartment window on a late May evening. Spring was on its way out and summer on its way in.

Isabel closed her hand around the rock she was using as a hopscotch marker on the sidewalk. Her friend Yoshiko stopped in mid-hop and turned her head. Isabel stood still and tilted her head back to see her brother hanging out of the fourth-floor front room window. Sitting on the front steps of the apartment, Steven also looked up.

"Mama says you should come in soon," Frank announced. "It's almost suppertime."

"But Daddy isn't even home yet," Isabel protested. She glanced down the street.

Frank turned his head for a moment, then looked back at Isabel. "Mama says ten more minutes."

"You should do what your mother asks," Yoshiko said. She narrowed her almond black eyes and looked sternly at Isabel. "It is not proper to show disrespect to your parents."

"Is that a Japanese proverb?" Isabel asked skeptically. She tossed her stone down in the box with a big *3* in it and started hopping.

Yoshiko shook her head. "Just common sense. You'll get into trouble sooner or later."

"You're probably right," Isabel agreed. She turned around at the end of the hopscotch board and started hopping back toward her stone.

"You should listen to your friend," Steven observed. "She makes sense."

"I didn't see you jumping up and running upstairs," Isabel retorted. She picked up her stone and finished her turn.

"But I will when it's time."

Yoshiko tossed her stone. It landed squarely in the box marked *4*.

Steven sprang to his feet. "Here comes Daddy now. And he has a newspaper!" He ran a few yards and reached for the paper folded securely under Daddy's left elbow. Steven intended to open the Seattle *Times* directly to the sports page, but the headline on the front page caught his attention.

"Hey! Did you see this?"

Daddy nodded. "I read it on the streetcar. A very sad story."

"What is it?" Isabel and Yoshiko wanted to know. They stopped their game and crowded around Steven to see the paper.

"George Weyerhaeuser was kidnapped," Steven reported.

"Who is George Weyerhaeuser?"

"You know, the Weyerhaeuser family," Steven said, "the people who own all the timber companies all over the Northwest."

"And a few other places, too," Daddy added. "George is just a little boy, just a little younger than you, Isabel. His family lives in Tacoma."

"And he was kidnapped?"

Daddy nodded and sighed.

"Because his family is rich?" Yoshiko asked.

Daddy nodded again. "I expect there will be a ransom demand. They'll want a lot of money before they will return George to his family."

"His family has a lot of money," Isabel said, "so they'll pay it, right?"

Daddy reached out and put his open palm gently against Isabel's cheek. "I know I would pay every penny I had to get one of my children back."

Isabel saw the sad look in her father's nearly black eyes and tried to imagine how George's family must be feeling. "I suppose even rich people love their children."

Daddy kissed the top of her head.

"How did they catch him?" Yoshiko wanted to know.

"Let's see," Steven said, opening the paper again, "it says here he left Lowell Grammar School to go home for lunch, but he never got there."

"Was he walking?" Isabel asked.

Steven nodded.

"If his family is so rich, why did he have to walk home from school like an ordinary kid? Why didn't they send the chauffeur to pick him up?"

Steven rolled his eyes. "Maybe his mother thought the

exercise would do him good. The point is, he was walking, and somebody else picked him up."

"Did someone see what happened?" Isabel asked.

Steven shook his head. "No. No witnesses have come forward. But he had to have been taken on his way home for lunch. His teacher said he was fine when he left the school building. They started looking for him right away, but it was too late." He studied the paper again. "It says here he was wearing a sweater, brown corduroy pants, and Keds tennis shoes. The police want everyone to be on the lookout for him."

As Steven folded the newspaper, Daddy shook his head sadly. "Just two years ago Charles Lindbergh's son was kidnapped."

Isabel's ears perked up. "Charles Lindbergh, the flyer?"

"Yes, that's right. He is famous for his skills as a pilot, but his family is also quite well to do. His small son was taken and found murdered. I hope the Weyerhaeusers will not have to go through that."

"Isabel!" Frank was bellowing out the window again. "Mama says to come right now!" Grinning, Frank waved at his father.

"We'll all be right up," Daddy called out, returning Frank's wave.

Isabel turned to Yoshiko. "Can you play later?"

"Come down as soon as you're through eating."

Before the Harrington family started eating, Daddy prayed for the safety of George Weyerhaeuser, as well as giving thanks for the food. Isabel only half-listened to the conversation at the supper table. She was getting an idea, and she needed all of her mental energy to work out the details. Fortunately, it was Alice's turn to help with the dishes. Isabel scraped her plate clean and asked to be excused.

She zipped downstairs to Yoshiko's apartment. Her friend

answered the door when she knocked.

"Are you finished eating? Can you play?"

"I suppose so," Yoshiko muttered. "But I don't really feel much like playing."

Isabel scowled. It was not like Yoshiko to be unhappy. What could have happened in the brief time since they'd been playing hopscotch together?

"What's wrong, Yoshiko?"

"I have to go to school," Yoshiko groaned. She threw herself down on a small sofa.

"But you already go to school. And in the fall, I'm going to go to school with you. We want to be in the same class, remember?"

Yoshiko shook her head. "No, you don't understand. My parents want me to go to Japanese school."

"Japanese school?"

"Yes. To learn Japanese language and culture."

Isabel scrunched up her face, puzzled. "Aren't you already Japanese? I hear you speaking Japanese to your parents all the time."

"No, they speak Japanese to me," Yoshiko responded, "and I answer in English. I don't really like speaking Japanese. Now I'm going to have to study Japanese and learn how to dress in Japanese clothes and bow to my elders and do tea ceremonies and all that stuff. My parents are afraid I don't appreciate my cultural heritage."

"You might like it," Isabel suggested.

Yoshiko screwed up her face. "Maybe you should go instead."

"I could go with you sometime," Isabel offered.

Yoshiko nodded. "That just might help. Then at least we could say we ate rice from the same pot."

"You have to go to a special school to eat rice?"

"It's an expression. It means we share an experience."

"So you do know some Japanese culture already."

"I can't believe I have to spend my whole summer taking Japanese classes."

"That won't take all your time, will it?" Isabel asked.

"No, but it will feel like it does."

"I was hoping you would have some time left over for some detective work."

"Detective work?"

Isabel nodded enthusiastically. "We can look for George Weyerhaeuser."

"Us? What can we do?" Yoshiko sat up straight on the sofa.

"My mother always tells me that you never know what you can do unless you try. So I think we should try."

"Shouldn't we let the police handle this?"

"You heard what Steven said. The police are asking everyone to keep a lookout for George Weyerhaeuser."

"Yes, but that doesn't mean we should try to catch the kidnappers ourselves."

"I'm not going to worry about the kidnappers," Isabel said, "I just want to find the little boy."

"How are you going to find George without worrying about the kidnappers?"

"I'll figure that out later. Are you going to help me?"

"So what do we need to do?" Yoshiko asked. She was warming up to the idea. Doing detective work had to be better than going to Japanese school.

"We'll need a headquarters," Isabel said authoritatively, "a central command post. It can't be in my apartment, because there are too many little kids there."

Yoshiko jumped up. "I know! There's an empty apartment

at the back of the first floor. The people who want to rent it don't want to move in till July."

"We'll only need it for a few days," Isabel said confidently. "I'm sure we'll find George before July. Lead me to our headquarters."

"Do we need anything else?"

Isabel pursed her lips thoughtfully. "The newspaper."

Yoshiko snatched the evening's paper from the coffee table. "Let's go." She marched ahead of Isabel out of the Wakamutsus' apartment and down the dim hall. The door was unlocked and opened easily.

Isabel scanned the room. It was empty except for two crates and a stack of cardboard boxes of various sizes. "This will be perfect. We'll be able to have confidential conversations in here while we talk about the clues of the case." She started rearranging the crates and boxes.

"Have we got any clues?"

"That's what the newspaper is for. We'll list the information we have so far."

"Well, we know what he was wearing and approximately what time he disappeared," Yoshiko reported.

"I think we can assume that the kidnappers had a car," Isabel added. "And they're going to want money. I'm sure there will be more information in the paper tomorrow."

Yoshiko turned her head toward the open apartment door. "Did you hear that?"

"What?" Isabel tilted her head to listen.

"It's Frank, calling for you."

Isabel's eyes lit up. She heard the muffled sound of her brother's voice. "Is he in the hall?"

"It sounds like he is."

Isabel put a finger to her lips and motioned that Yoshiko

should follow her. They crept out into the darkened hallway. Isabel could see Frank's silhouette in the light at the other end of the hall.

"Isabel? Mama is looking for you." Frank turned his head from left to right looking for his sister.

With her back pressed up against the wall, Isabel inched sideways toward her brother. He had his back turned toward her and was moving toward the Wakamutsus' apartment. He knocked on the door and waited patiently. Yoshiko's seven-year-old brother, Kaneko, answered the door. Isabel covered her mouth to smother her giggle as she saw Kaneko answer Frank's question by shaking his head.

Yoshiko, suspecting what Isabel was planning, gave her a stern look. Isabel ignored her.

Frank sighed and turned toward the stairs. Isabel slid smoothly and silently along the wall. Before Frank could put his foot on the first step, Isabel pounced and poked her fingers into the back of his ribs. Frank jumped about four inches off the floor and yelped like a wounded puppy.

Isabel roared with laughter.

"Isabel Harrington, you are so mean!" Frank's face was beet red and he whirled to face her.

Isabel stifled her laughter and tried to look sorry. But she wasn't.

CHAPTER 13

The Investigation

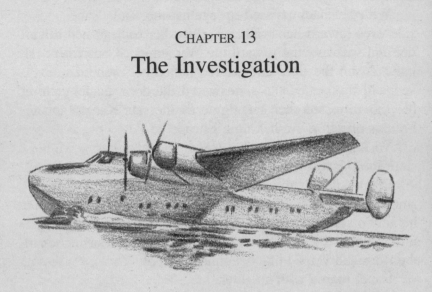

For days the headlines in Seattle and across the nation blared the news of young George Weyerhaeuser's disappearance. Reporters had many theories, but the plain fact was that no one knew what had happened to him.

Isabel felt sorry for George, of course, but she could not help being fascinated by all the efforts to find him. It seemed that no one in the neighborhood wanted to talk about anything else. Every evening after supper, Isabel and Yoshiko met in the empty apartment to go over the evidence again.

Frank had learned to stay out of their way. If Mama sent him to find Isabel, he called loudly from the other end of the hall. "I know you're down there," he would say. "If you don't come, then you'll get in trouble with Mama, and it will be your own fault."

On Saturday, four days after the kidnapping, Isabel slunk into the room to find Yoshiko waiting for her as usual. Isabel perched a baseball cap on her head sideways.

"What have we got tonight?" she asked in her most official tone. She took her seat on an overturned crate behind a desk made of two boxes and a board stretched between them.

Yoshiko opened the shoe box that contained everything they had gathered during the investigation. She began sorting the newspaper clippings. One by one, she laid them on the makeshift desk in a neat row.

"We'd better review what we already know," Yoshiko said. "Maybe we missed something. You never know when something will jump out at us."

Isabel crossed her legs and nodded seriously.

"First, no one saw the kidnapping," Yoshiko said. "Do you believe that's really possible in a town like Tacoma? George can't have been the only kid walking home for lunch."

Isabel shook her head. "I don't know what to think about that. Even in a city with a lot of people around, people don't always pay attention to what's going on around them."

"The family received a ransom note the very first night George was missing."

Isabel nodded. "Right. The kidnappers want $200,000. And they are probably going to get it."

"Right, because to the Weyerhaeusers, $200,000 is like fish grinding their teeth."

"Another Japanese expression?" Isabel asked suspiciously.

"It means that it's of no consequence. It means very little."

Isabel nodded. "I like that one."

"We have a lot of background information about the Weyerhaeuser family," Yoshiko continued. "George's grandfather, John Philip Weyerhaeuser, died recently."

"That was in the news," Isabel said. "Anyone could have known about it."

"Do you think that's important?"

"It might be."

"The family lives in a mansion on Fourth Street in Tacoma."

"That probably doesn't matter much," Isabel observed. "This could have happened just as well if they lived in Seattle."

"I didn't know people could be so rich." Yoshiko picked up a clipping with photographs showing the family home and a Weyerhaeuser paper mill. "My parents own this building, but the Weyerhaeusers own property in Washington, Oregon, Idaho, Arkansas, Vermont, Oklahoma, and a bunch of other places."

"The criminals knew what they were doing when they picked George Weyerhaeuser."

Yoshiko picked up another clipping. "Here's one that quotes his barber. He says that George was a manly little man."

"That's a silly expression," Isabel snickered. "He's just saying it because George is missing."

Yoshiko picked up another clipping. "His teacher at Lowell Grammar School says he was alert, obedient, and a brilliant pupil."

"She has to say something nice to the newspaper reporters. It would be horribly mean to say something nasty about a boy who has been kidnapped."

Yoshiko looked up. "So you don't think George is a good student?"

"I'm just saying it makes no difference. Have you ever been to a funeral? People say nice things, even if the person who died was truly awful."

"I suppose so. Then do you think we know anything important?"

"Is there anything there about what the police think?" Isabel leaned forward on her crate and looked at her friend intently.

"This one says that the kidnappers are part of a mob from the Midwest, something called the Karpis Gang."

Isabel nodded thoughtfully, even though she had never heard of the Karpis Gang.

"One psychiatrist thinks that the ransom note was written by a well-educated person, a college graduate. But another psychiatrist says the kidnapper is somebody who is not very intelligent."

"Well, they can't both be right," Isabel said firmly.

Yoshiko shrugged. "I guess the experts don't really know any more than we do."

"Then George Weyerhaeuser is in more trouble than we think."

A shadow appeared in the open apartment door.

"Here you are," Steven said. He walked right in, kicking a box as he approached Isabel.

Isabel scowled. "We're busy."

Steven laughed. "Sure you are. You're not going to find George Weyerhaeuser by sitting in this room reading newspaper clippings."

"We know a lot more about the case than you do."

"I know plenty," Steven said in his own defense. "But what I really want to know is how the Indians are doing. You snuck off with the newspaper again tonight before I got a chance to read it."

"I'll give you the sports section," Isabel said, flipping through the newspaper.

"You know, sometimes other people want to read the paper, too," Steven said. "I know Alice wants to see it."

"What part does she want?" Isabel was not convinced she should give away the whole newspaper just yet.

Steven shrugged. "She's interested in the international news, stuff about Europe. She wants to know what's happening."

"That's all the way across the ocean. We don't live in Europe," Isabel said, "so it doesn't matter much to us."

"Don't let Mama hear you talk that way," Steven warned. "Mama and Daddy remember the Great War. What happens in Europe might someday matter to us again."

"There isn't going to be another world war," Isabel insisted. "I hear people say that all the time on the radio." She laid the newspaper out on the floor and began turning the pages. "You can tell Alice that there's nothing about Europe in the paper today."

"Maybe she'd like to see for herself."

"I'm using the paper right now." Isabel stopped flipping and widened her eyes. "Look, there's an article about the Pan Am China Clipper."

"What's that?" Yoshiko asked.

"Pan Am has a plane that can fly across an ocean. They call it a flying boat."

"Fly across an ocean?" Yoshiko echoed in disbelief.

Isabel nodded enthusiastically. "It has beds and dinner tables and everything you need, just like a ship. They give you a fancy dinner on tablecloths and get your bed ready for you."

"I'm not allowed to touch my mother's tablecloths," Yoshiko said, "and I have to fix my own bed every day."

Isabel snickered. "When we first stayed in your hotel, you even had to fix my bed."

"That's as close as you'll ever get to a flying boat."

"Unless, of course, I'm the pilot. I suppose only people like

106

the Weyerhaeusers can actually afford to fly across oceans."

"Does Boeing have a plane like that?" Yoshiko asked.

Isabel shook her head. "Not yet. But I'm sure they will someday."

"If they finish building bombers, that is," Steven said.

"Your father is working on building a plane with bombs?" Yoshiko asked.

Isabel nodded proudly. "Yes, the 299. It's quite a plane."

"But why do they need to build bombers if there isn't going to be another world war?"

"It's one way to make sure that no one starts a war," Isabel said. She got up off the floor to get the cramp out of her leg. "The whole world will know that the United States has the 299 bomber. So no one will dare do anything to make us mad."

"Do you think that really works?" Yoshiko asked.

Isabel shrugged. "That's what the army thinks." She sat back down on her crate and rubbed her leg.

"I see you're finished with the paper." As he spoke, Steven dove to the floor, scooped up the newspaper, and scrambled for the door.

"Hey!" Isabel protested. But it was too late. Steven had what he wanted and was gone.

"It's okay," Yoshiko said. "There wasn't anything new in it anyway."

Isabel pouted. "Steven is right, you know. We'll never find George sitting in this room waiting for the clues to come to us. We have to get out in the field and dig up some new information ourselves."

Yoshiko stared at her friend. "Just how do you plan to do that?"

Isabel shrugged. "We'll have to go to Tacoma, to the scene of the crime."

107

"Do you know how far away Tacoma is?"

"I know it's too far to walk or ride a bicycle. But there must be a streetcar or a train or something."

"Have you ever been to Tacoma before?"

"I've only been in Seattle a little more than three weeks," Isabel answered. "But now that you mention it, it's time to explore some new territory."

"You're being silly. We'd get horribly lost."

"So you've never been to Tacoma, either?"

"Nope."

"I'm sure we could ask directions."

"What about money for the car fare or train ticket?"

"I used to know a hobo who rode trains all over the country and never bought a ticket."

"If you get caught, you could be in a lot of trouble."

Isabel glowered at her friend. "Must you be so practical? Don't you want to help poor George?"

"Of course I want to help George. But there isn't really anything we can do."

"I'm not going to sit here and do nothing." Isabel stomped out of the apartment and down the front hall. She shoved open the front door to the building and stood on the sidewalk with her hands on her hips. She looked down the street and up the street. She hated to admit it, but she had no idea which way Tacoma was. Steven probably would know, but Isabel had no intention of letting Steven find out that she did not know which way was south and which was north.

Yoshiko came up behind her. "Now what?"

Isabel turned her head and looked at her friend. "I thought you weren't coming."

"I can't let you go alone."

Isabel scanned the sky, hiding her relief. "Well, it's getting too late to go today, anyway. Maybe tomorrow, after church."

"Yes, maybe tomorrow," Yoshiko agreed. She brightened. "My mother is very glad that your family is going to visit our church."

"We always go to church," Isabel said. "If the doors are open, the Harringtons are there. Mama says we just need to find the right church in Seattle."

"I'm not sure you will want to keep coming to our church."

"Why not? It sounds like a good church."

"We have many Japanese families in our church," Yoshiko explained. "Perhaps you will feel uncomfortable there."

"I don't know what you're talking about," Isabel said. "I'm sure it's a perfectly fine church."

Yoshiko smiled. "Tomorrow you will find out what it is like to look around and not see any faces that look like yours."

"Mama says the way people look doesn't matter, and I think she's right."

Yoshiko nodded. "Your mother is very wise. But many people will be speaking Japanese. You might not understand very much."

"You'll be there to translate."

"Isabel!" Frank's voice blew down from the window above them. "Mama says come in!"

CHAPTER 14
Baseball School

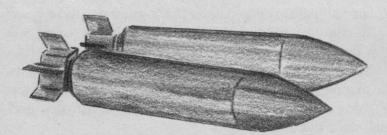

"I didn't really want to come, you know," Isabel said as she pumped her legs to keep pace with Steven. "I'm not very interested in baseball. It was Mama's idea for me to come."

"You're not going to complain all afternoon, are you?" Steven asked, without slowing down.

"I'm not complaining, I'm just remarking." She took her hands out of her overall pockets and swung them along her sides to increase her speed.

"Don't worry, you don't have to play," Steven responded. "You can just watch."

"What's the point of going to a baseball clinic and just watching?"

"Suit yourself," Steven said, losing patience. "Mama just

wanted you to get outside for a while. You've been spending too much time in that empty apartment with Yoshiko."

"We were working on a case."

"Yeah, well, the case is over now. George Weyerhaeuser is back home, safe and sound. The police caught the kidnappers. So you can call off the hunt."

"Steven Harrington, don't you make fun of me!"

"I would never think of such a thing," Steven said dryly. "Sooner or later, I'm sure you would have figured out that the kidnappers were not an organized gang, but just three greedy people with a mean streak. It's unfortunate that the police beat you to it."

"Stop it, Steven, I'm warning you! Besides, the police didn't really solve it. The kidnappers kept George until they got their money. One of them was really nice to George. That sportswriter you like so much wrote about it in the *Post Intelligencer.*"

"He's just a golf writer who got a lucky break," Steven said.

"But you have to admit, the police did not solve the case until they got more information from George."

Steven ignored his sister's indignation. "Look around, Isabel. You've never been to this part of Seattle before. You might even see something you like."

"I'm sure Civic Field is just another baseball field," Isabel answered. "I've seen a thousand."

Steven looked at her sideways. "A thousand? I bet you can't name three."

Isabel stuck her nose up in the air. "I could if I wanted to. But I don't see the point."

"I'm looking forward to this baseball clinic. You can just enjoy the sun for a couple hours."

Steven's steps slowed as they finally approached Civic

Field. The truth is that it wasn't much of a baseball park. It looked more like an abandoned lot. With its run-down fences and rickety seats, it hardly seemed like the kind of place where a professional baseball team would play.

"I heard that Dugdale Park was a terrific baseball park," Steven said wistfully as he surveyed Civic Field. Even he was disappointed with what he saw.

"So why don't the Indians play there?" Isabel asked.

"It burned down three years ago," Steven answered. "But they're going to build a new stadium, and it will be even better than Dugdale Park."

"How do you know that? You never saw Dugdale Park."

Steven rolled his eyes. "Let's just go in."

They went through the gate and found themselves standing in the infield. The inside of the park looked just as bad as the outside, maybe even worse. There was no grass, even in the outfield. Dust clouds blew up with every step anyone took. The dirt was cluttered with small rocks. Hidden holes could trip even the best runner. But the hundreds of kids inside the park did not seem to mind the surroundings. The free baseball school had already started. Excited to be there, many of the kids were screeching and yelling and not paying much attention to what they were supposed to do.

"Why don't you find a place to sit?" Steven said. "You have your choice of sun or shade."

Isabel tilted her head and stuck out her lower lip. "No, I think I'll see what this is all about."

"I thought you didn't like baseball."

"I don't. But as long as I'm here, I might as well join in. You said yourself I might like it."

"I don't see very many other girls," Steven said, scanning the crowd.

"That doesn't matter one bit. If I want to do it, I'll do it."

The group, nearly all boys dressed in sweatshirts and crooked caps, Keds and pants worn in the knees, swarmed around the instructors. About a dozen adults were trying to organize them into groups to work on baseball skills. It was not an easy task.

"Hey, that's Tubby Graves!" Steven said excitedly.

"Who's Tubby Graves?"

Steven looked at his sister and scowled. "If you ever listened to anything I said at home, you would know who Tubby Graves is."

"Oh, you mean the man from the University of Washington?"

Steven sighed in exasperation.

"He coaches the baseball team, right?" Isabel continued.

"If you knew all that, why did you act like you didn't know who he was?" Steven wanted to know.

Isabel shrugged and grinned. Steven looked away from her to see Tubby Graves moving toward the left-field fence. He had several bats clutched in his fists.

"Over here!" Tubby hollered. His voice easily carried across the park. "Over here by the fence, we're going to learn how to hit."

"I'm going over there," Steven said. "You do what you want to do."

Tubby Graves was a big man, with huge feet and slouching shoulders. His voice was loud but friendly. He swung a bat in his enormous hands while a couple dozen kids gathered around him.

"Let's imagine," Tubby said, "that you've just cornered the Weyerhaeuser kidnapper. You're gonna hit the Weyerhaeuser kidnapper in the belly. Let me show you how you're gonna do it."

113

Tubby took up a tight batting stance and held the bat over his shoulder. "There's his belly. Now swing! No fancy stuff, just wham!" He swung the bat to demonstrate. It swished violently through the air.

Everyone in the park knew about the Weyerhaeuser case. Every kid in the group instantly understood how to swing the bat to hit the kidnapper in the belly, and they were eager to do it.

Isabel confidently stepped up to join the group. She was the only girl, but she did not care. If she had not been able to catch the kidnappers herself, the least she could do was imagine she was punishing them. Steven swung his bat vigorously, concentrating on every movement of his body.

"Okay," Tubby said, "now you've got it. Let's hit some real balls."

The players lined up to take turns batting at the balls Tubby Graves pitched to them. Isabel did not think that swinging at real baseballs was nearly as much fun. She lagged behind the others, not caring whether or not she got her turn to hit. Her mind wandered.

Daddy was working a lot of overtime. Boeing was trying to win a contract with the army for a bomber that could travel more than 200 miles per hour and carry 2,000 pounds of bombs. If they got the contract, they would build 220 planes. Daddy's job would be secure for a long time. But the first plane, as an example of what Boeing could build, would have to be ready in August. It was already the beginning of June. The army had not given them much time, and several other companies were also racing to meet the deadline.

Daddy seemed to like his job at Boeing. His experience designing machines at the Pillsbury Mill in Minneapolis gave him a good understanding of the way parts of a plane must work together. And Isabel thought designing airplanes was far more interesting than working on flour mill machinery. She tried not to nag too much, but she never let her father forget that he had promised to take her to Boeing for a tour and to see the new bomber.

Mama did not want to go on the tour. Or at least she did not want to see the bomber. She was glad Daddy was working. But she seemed a little nervous that he was working on planes that could drop bombs to destroy whole towns and kill a lot of people. Isabel had asked her mother about it only a few days ago, when Daddy was once again late coming home from work.

"I just don't like the idea of bombs," Mama had said.

"But Daddy says the planes probably won't ever have to be used for bombs," Isabel said, repeating what her father had told her several times. "It's just to let other countries know we could do it if we wanted to. But we wouldn't want to."

Mama was not satisfied with that explanation. "The army is spending a lot of money on something they say they won't need."

"Isn't it better to have it and not need it than to need it and not have it?" Isabel asked.

Mama's face clouded over. She reached out to stroke the side of Isabel's face.

"The Great War caused so much destruction," she said quietly, "and there was so much hate. It was a difficult time to be German."

"That's not going to happen again. Everybody says that was the war to end all wars."

"I truly hope so," Mama said. "I pray every day that you children will never experience what I saw as a child. I just hate the thought that your father's work might have something to do with that happening again."

"Boeing is working on some other planes, too," Isabel reminded her mother. "Some people just want to be able to fly across the ocean to visit other countries, not to bomb them."

Mama had smiled then. "Now that's my kind of plane."

Isabel leaned on a bat in left field as she thought about that conversation with her mother. Mama hardly ever seemed afraid of anything. Leaving Minneapolis and her friends and family, traveling all the way across the country without enough money, even setting up housekeeping in a new city—none of that had bothered Mama. But whenever anyone talked about the war, Mama got really quiet. Even though the war had been over for almost twenty years, Mama remembered everything about it.

"Little lady, are you going to swing or not?"

It was Tubby Graves, motioning that Isabel should step up and take her turn. Isabel considered walking away, but then she remembered the Weyerhaeuser kidnapper.

When the pitch came, she swung and whacked the air where she was sure the kidnapper's belly should have been. Mama and Daddy probably would disapprove of the imagined violence, but it was a good way to learn to hit a pitch. To Isabel's satisfaction, the ball sailed over the heads of all the boys.

CHAPTER 15
A Fruitless Search

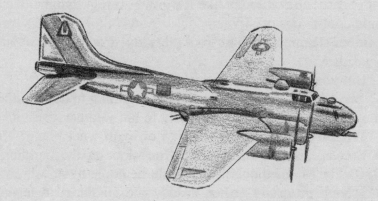

"Was this the day? Was this the day?"

At the sight of her father walking up the sidewalk, Isabel hopped off the stoop and dashed toward him. She had waited most of the day for this moment.

"Did they do it today?" she asked, tugging on Daddy's arm. She fell into step beside him, easily keeping pace with his relaxed saunter.

Daddy smiled and nodded. "This was the day, all right."

"I want to hear everything, every little detail. Don't leave anything out."

Daddy laughed. "If only the executives at Boeing could

see your enthusiasm. They would hire you in a flash. Anybody with your excitement deserves to work for the company that builds the best planes in the world."

They reached the front of their apartment building. Daddy sat down on the stoop and took off his hat.

"I don't care about any silly executive," Isabel exclaimed. "I just want to know about the plane."

"It's mighty hot," Daddy commented, raising his eyes to the waning sun. "Somehow I did not expect summer to be so hot in Seattle. But it looks like it's going to rain tonight. That should cool things off."

Isabel stamped her bare foot. "Daddy! I don't care about the weather."

"But you would agree that it's hot."

"Yes, it's hot, but that doesn't have anything to do with the plane, does it? The plane can still fly in hot weather, can't it?"

"What doesn't have anything to do with what plane?" It was Steven, just coming out the front door of the building. "Hi, Daddy. Mama thought you might be home by now."

"I should go up and see her," Daddy said. He started to get up.

"No!" Isabel threw herself into her father's lap, nearly knocking him over. "You can't go until you tell me about the plane."

"What plane?" Steven repeated his question.

Isabel sighed in exasperation. "Don't you pay attention to anything? Daddy's been working on building a new plane for the army ever since we got here."

"Oh, that plane."

Daddy chuckled. "Let's not get ahead of ourselves," he said to Isabel. "We've only designed a prototype. That means it's just a sample of what we might build. We don't know yet if the army is going to choose our plane."

118

"But it's a real plane, isn't it?"

"Absolutely."

"And this was the day, wasn't it? You said it was."

"What day?" Steven asked, a glint of humor in his eyes.

Isabel ignored him. "Did they fly the plane or not?"

Daddy nodded. "Yes, ma'am, they did. They towed that machine down the Duwamish River and put it in the air. Mr. Les Tower flew the 299 for the first time on this day, July 28, 1935."

"Wow! I wish I could have been there. Can I go with you the next time? I can hardly imagine a plane that's nearly 104 feet across the wingspan. That's clear into the next block from here. And it's 32,432 pounds. Does a whole building even weigh that much? And with four engines, it can get up in the air lickety-split. Can it really go 236 miles per hour, like it's supposed to?"

Daddy was grinning. "I can see you've been studying up. You know more about it than many people who work in the Boeing plant. I didn't know you were paying such close attention to all of my mumblings."

"I listen to everything you say—if you're talking about planes, that is. I can't wait until I can take a trip in a plane myself. I'm even going to learn to fly one. I could even learn to fly the 299. As a matter of fact, I would really like that. Do you think the army will allow girl pilots?"

Daddy gently nudged Isabel from his lap and stood up. "Don't worry about what the army will allow, Isabel. Just decide what you want to do and then do it!"

"Someday I'm going to fly a plane," she said emphatically.

"You don't have to be in the army for that," Steven reminded her. "Boeing has other planes, like the Clippers that fly to Europe. They carry passengers, not bombs."

Isabel nodded. "Yes, I suppose that would be better. Mama would not be so worried."

"Speaking of Mama," Daddy said, "I'm going to go on up and say hello. You two come in for supper, okay?"

"We'll be up in a few minutes," Steven promised.

Steven sunk down onto the stoop, sweating. "I wish there was someplace close where we could go swimming," he said. "It's so hot! All we have is that one little fan in the kitchen. It's so feeble, I don't know why Mama bothers to turn it on."

"The Wakamutsus are planning to rent a cottage at the beach," Isabel said. "They'll be gone for the whole month of August—except Mr. Wakamutsu. He says he has too much work to do here."

"Someone has to keep an eye on things," Steven said. "It's hard to take a vacation when you have your own business."

"I'm hoping that Yoshiko will invite me for a few days," Isabel continued. "I know she wants to. She'll be there with her mother and her brothers. I promised her I wouldn't be any trouble. I could even take my own food. But she has to talk to her mother about it first."

"August starts in three days," Steven observed. "Are you sure they have a cottage to rent?"

"They're still looking. Oh, here they come!" Isabel was again on her feet. Mrs. Wakamutsu, Yoshiko, and the two little Wakamutsu boys straggled across the street. When they reached Isabel, Mrs. Wakamutsu smiled thinly. Isabel thought she looked very tired.

"Hello, Mrs. Wakamutsu," Steven said politely.

"Hello, Steven, Isabel. Excuse me. I must go inside now."

Before Isabel or Steven could say anything else, Mrs. Wakamutsu took her two sons by the hands and smoothly disappeared through the front door.

Isabel turned to greet Yoshiko, who straggled behind. "Is your mother all right?"

Yoshiko raised an arm to wipe the dripping sweat from her face. "It was a very long day," she said, "and it did not go as well as we hoped."

"Do you mean you still couldn't find a cottage to rent?"

Yoshiko shook her head. "We saw a 'for rent' sign on a beautiful cottage this morning. We could hardly believe that it was still available. But we could see through the windows that no one was living in it. So we asked about it."

"And?"

"They said it was rented, and they had forgotten to take the sign out of the window."

"You sound like you don't believe that," Steven said.

Yoshiko shrugged. "It was the same cottage we saw a month ago. The owner told us then that it was rented for the whole summer. So why was it empty today?"

"Maybe somebody had it for July and they had to leave a few days early," Isabel said.

Yoshiko shook her head wearily. "No. They did not want to rent it to us because we are Japanese." Tears glimmered in her dark eyes.

"That can't be true!" Isabel protested.

"But it is true," Yoshiko cried. "You don't understand what it is like to be Japanese in a city where everyone else is white."

"What difference does that make?" Isabel asked.

"Imagine if you lived in Japan," Yoshiko said. "What if your whole life was like the day you visited my church?"

"It wouldn't matter," Isabel insisted.

But Steven understood. "I suppose you looked at several cottages," he said.

Yoshiko nodded. "And it was always the same. They were all rented, but the owners had forgotten to take the sign down. You would think they could at least come up with a better excuse than that." She turned to Isabel. "There is no reason to ask my mother if you can join us for a few days. We will be right here all through the hottest days of August. I'm sure I'll see you every day."

"You can't give up now," Isabel exclaimed.

Yoshiko shrugged. "My mother is tired. It is not easy to be Japanese."

"But you're not Japanese. You're American."

"I have a Japanese face. So I am Japanese. My parents are not citizens, and I am their daughter. Besides, we have looked at everything. No one wants us." Yoshiko glanced toward the door and wiped her eyes with one hand. "I should go see if my mother wants help preparing supper. She was hoping to have a celebration tonight, but now it will be an ordinary meal."

Yoshiko dragged her feet up the steps and through the door. It slammed shut behind her.

When Yoshiko had gone, Isabel sunk down on the stoop next to Steven. "The Wakamutsus are a nice family. Yoshiko is probably the best friend I've ever had. Why are people being so mean?"

"It's very complicated," Steven said.

"Well, try to explain it to me," Isabel insisted. "I want to understand."

"It has to do with international politics," Steven said.

"Yoshiko doesn't have anything to do with politics," Isabel said. "She's a ten-year-old girl, just like me."

"But she's Japanese."

"No, she's American."

"She looks Japanese."

"I don't understand what you're trying to say, Steven."

"I like Yoshiko as much as you do. You have to understand that. I think it's interesting to have as many Japanese neighbors as we have. In Minneapolis, everybody looked European. This is much more interesting."

"But?"

"But not everybody feels that way. The Japanese—the country, I mean—are doing some things that make a lot of people nervous."

"Like what?"

"Like trying to take over China. According to Alice, the emperor of China is just a puppet for the Japanese. He does everything they want him to do."

"That doesn't have anything to do with the Wakamutsus," Isabel insisted. "They don't even live in Japan, and if they did, they still would have nothing to do with the government."

"I know that, and you know that. But don't forget about all the stories Mama has told about how hard it was to grow up German."

Isabel nodded. "Everything was so hard for Grandpa and Grandma—and for Mama."

"Some people just can't see past a name like Schmidt or a face with slanted eyes. They don't like to have anybody around who is not exactly the same as they are."

"Well, that's just silly."

"I think so, too," Steven said, "but that's not going to help the Wakamutsus get a summer cottage at the beach. It's not going to help Mr. Wakamutsu get the kind of engineering job he's qualified for so he can stop sweeping sidewalks and making beds. But it's reality."

"Then I don't like reality. We have to change reality."

"That's a big job."

The door creaked open behind them. It was Frank. "Mama says to come to supper."

CHAPTER 16

Serious Thoughts

Civic Field in the middle of August was a busy place. The Seattle Indians were a minor league team and played in a humble stadium, but they had loyal fans who filled every seat in the park. The days were hot, but true-blooded baseball fans did not mind. They came to see the Indians play, rain or shine, breeze or heat blast.

Steven had been scraping his coins together all summer to have enough to ride the streetcar to Queen Anne Hill and buy a ticket for a baseball game. He had listened to many of the summer's games on the radio and knew all the players' names, numbers, and positions. Now he would get to see their faces. Some of them were ready to move up to a major league team, and he wanted to see them play before they did that.

The fence around the park was weathered and splintered in many places. Some of the planks hung by only one nail. Even the posts were rotted at the base where they went into the ground. Steven could easily have snuck in by moving a loose board and squeezing through the fence. He had heard other boys talking about doing that. Some of the boys in his neighborhood went to two games every week without ever paying a cent. But Steven proudly marched up to the ticket booth and paid for his entrance. He did not want anything, especially a guilty conscience, to spoil this occasion for him.

His seat was right along the first base line. From there, he would have a clear view of everything that happened during the game. He could study the pitcher's form as he wound up and hurtled the ball at unbelievable speeds. He could hear the crack of the bat as it met the ball—or the swoosh through the air if the batter missed. He could see the umpire's thumb as he ruled that the runner trying to steal second base was out.

Steven had come to the field for the free baseball clinic in June, but this was his first real baseball game since leaving Minneapolis. He was keeping track of every play in the game on a sheet of paper torn from his mother's notebook. Later on, he was going to try to retell the game to Mama. She had never really understood baseball until Steven had started to follow the sport.

How anyone could grow up in the United States and not learn to play baseball was a mystery to Steven. But it had happened to Mama. Fortunately she never considered herself too old to learn something new. She was Steven's biggest fan, even though she had never seen a professional game herself.

Daddy was once again working long hours at Boeing, trying to make the 299 perfect for its flight to Ohio in a few days. Steven doubted his father would be home when the game was over. If Boeing got the contract for more planes, then Daddy would be busier than ever.

Alice understood baseball but said she had outgrown it. It was a child's game, she said, and at fourteen she was no longer a child. When Steven pointed out that grown men played the game, Alice only insisted that they only proved men were childish.

Isabel had seemed to have a good time at the baseball clinic, whacking at the kidnapper's belly as hard as she could. But she said baseball was too slow and took too long to play. Frank, at seven years old, was Steven's hope for the future. He considered it his responsibility to make sure Frank learned to understand the game. Steven regretted that he had not been able to save enough money for two tickets.

A batter struck out. Steven dutifully marked it on his page. Maybe next time he could bring Frank with him to the game. He ought to take more of an interest in Frank, he told himself. Isabel teased him entirely too much, and Frank fell for her tricks every time. Frank got carried away with having fun and rarely saw that Isabel was beginning to make fun of him until it was too late. An older brother could help Frank learn to see the clues that Isabel was up to something.

Squinting into the sun as a batter flied out to left field—right where Tubby Graves had swung at the Weyerhaeuser kidnapper—Steven considered the different personalities among his siblings. He admired Alice, except for her attitude about baseball. When the family needed money, she pitched in and got a job. She never once complained about handing over all her earnings to Mama for groceries.

Audrey was a worrier. She had fussed about her wagon and her dolls all the way across the country. But even at five years old, it was obvious that Audrey would grow up to be an organizer. She would make sure everything was in its rightful place and taken care of properly. Now that she was learning to read under Mama's guidance, Audrey was becoming more curious every day.

Even the twins, with the same curly dark hair topping their heads, were very different from each other. Ed was going to have to be careful not to let Barbara take over his life when they got older. She did everything first, and he followed.

Frank would believe anything anybody told him. He seemed to get sick a lot, and he had learned to do as he was told so he could get better. Isabel, on the other hand, refused to believe what she did not like to hear. Halfway through August, she had insisted that the Wakamutsus should not give up trying to find a beach cottage to rent. And it was no use talking to her about what was going on in Japan or in Europe. She would only say that none of it made any sense, and certainly none of it had anything to do with Yoshiko's family.

The next batter looped a ball over the second baseman's head into short right field. He easily made it to first base before the right fielder caught the ball on a bounce. Steven marked the play on his paper.

He hated what was going on in Europe. Isabel could pretend it didn't matter, because she was only ten. But Steven, almost fourteen, knew better. It did matter, and it mattered very much.

It was hard not to eavesdrop in their small apartment, especially when his assigned sleeping space was in the living room. Two nights ago he had heard his parents talking in the kitchen late at night. Mama did not like that Adolf Hitler was chancellor of Germany. He was a Nazi, and the Nazis could be just as ignorant and self-centered as the people who would not rent a cottage to the Wakamutsus. Hitler wanted everyone to be just like he was.

That's what Mama said, and Steven thought she was right. Hitler was making it illegal for Jews to live in Germany. Mama had cried when she heard that. That would be like telling the Wakamutsus they could not live in Seattle just because they were Japanese. Isabel would say that was stupid, and she would be right.

The next batter struck out, the third out for the inning. The Indian outfielders trotted in toward the dugout. As Steven marked the play, he wondered if Alice was right. Perhaps it was childish for grown men to be playing baseball. Maybe they should be paying more attention to what was happening in Japan and Germany. But then, what could the men who played on the Seattle Indians or any of the other teams really do to change the way Adolf Hitler thought? Absolutely nothing, Steven told himself. The people who lived in Germany would have to be the ones to change their government.

The Indians were up to bat now. Steven pushed thoughts of international politics out of his mind and focused on what he had come to Civic Field to see. Poised on the edge of his seat, he leaped to his feet when the first crack of the bat brought a home run.

CHAPTER 17
Bad News

Isabel tumbled through the door of the Harrington apartment and collapsed on the sofa, laughing. Yoshiko was right behind Isabel, her face split in two by a wide grin. She plopped down on the sofa next to Isabel.

"Do you mind?" Steven said indignantly. He sat in a chair across the room with a book open in his lap. "I'm trying to read in here. Take your party somewhere else."

Isabel stood up and bowed. "Oh, yes, most honorable brother. We do not wish to disturb you." She bowed again.

Steven raised his eyes to inspect his sister. "What's gotten into you?"

"Most honorable brother, I wish only to please you."

Steven wrinkled his forehead. "I don't know what you're scheming now, Isabel, but you're not going to get away with it. If you try to pull something on Frank—"

Isabel shook her head. "Oh, no, most noble brother. I have no scheme."

Yoshiko burst into laughter, and Isabel fell onto the sofa once again.

Mama came in from the kitchen, wiping her hands on a dishtowel. The twins straggled behind her.

"Oh, good, you're home," Mama said. "I want to hear all about Japanese school."

Steven groaned. "So that's what this is about, all this most-noble-brother talk."

Isabel grinned. "I had a great time, Mama."

"Are you going to visit the school again?"

"I don't think the teacher will let me do that!"

"I hope you didn't interfere with the class."

Isabel glanced at Yoshiko.

"She didn't exactly interfere," Yoshiko explained. "But she was a very curious student. Mrs. Mori didn't appreciate that."

"You were just supposed to observe, Isabel," Mama said. Barbara tugged on her leg and Mama stooped to pick her up.

"Bel-bel," Barbie said, pointing.

"I'm afraid Bel-bel has been naughty," Mama said.

"Oh, no," said Yoshiko. "She didn't do anything wrong. She just didn't do things exactly right."

Steven put his book down. "If I know Isabel, she had her own idea about how to run the class."

"I just had some questions, that's all. Yoshiko has been going to Japanese school since June. This is the end of October. I had some catching up to do."

"Catching up?" Mama said. "You were just supposed to watch."

"It's not that kind of a class, Mama," Isabel said in her own defense. "You have to get up and do things."

"Like bowing?" Steven speculated.

Isabel pressed her hands together and bowed with elegance.

"She learns quickly," Yoshiko said, smiling.

"I don't think Mrs. Mori wanted me there at all," Isabel said. "She hardly looked at me, even after Mrs. Wakamutsu introduced me as Yoshiko's friend. And I didn't understand much of what she said."

"That's because she was speaking Japanese, silly," Yoshiko said. "You didn't expect the teacher of a Japanese school to speak English to you, did you?"

"Well, I don't speak Japanese, and you said she does speak English."

Yoshiko shook her head. "Not during class. When you walk through those doors, everything is Japanese. You might as well be in Japan."

Isabel giggled. "I guess that explains why everyone there was Japanese. That was the strangest part of all."

"What do you mean?" Mama asked. Now Eddie wanted to be picked up. Mama handed Barb to Isabel and picked up Ed.

"Do you remember the day we visited Yoshiko's church?"

Mama nodded. "We were the only Caucasians there, except the pastor."

"And everybody looked at us funny," Steven added.

"That's what this was like," Isabel said. "It was as if I had no business being there, even just to find out what it's like to be Japanese."

"That's because most people don't care what it's like to be

Japanese," Yoshiko said. "You're the only Caucasian visitor we've had at Japanese school."

"I can't help it that I'm curious."

"I'm glad you are," Mama said. "And Grandpa and Grandma Schmidt would be proud of you, too. You would have welcomed them with open arms when they came from Germany."

Steven sniffed the air. "What's that smell?"

"Oh! Supper!" Mama abruptly set Eddie down and scurried to the kitchen. The girls followed. Isabel carried Barbara, and Yoshiko picked up Ed.

"Did you burn supper?" Isabel asked.

Mama moved a hot pan from the stove to the counter. "Not quite. But that was a close call."

"What are we having?"

"Alice found a bargain on some day-old vegetables at Pike Place Market this morning," Mama said. "I've boiled them, and I'm going to make some noodles."

"I wish we could have noodles the way Mrs. Wakamutsu makes it," Isabel said, looking at her friend. "Why are her noodles so much better than ordinary noodles?"

"My mother makes her own noodles," Yoshiko explained.

"Mrs. Wakamutsu is a very good cook. I'm sure I could learn a few things from her," Mama said.

"Do you want to learn how to cook Japanese food?" Yoshiko asked. "My mother could teach you. She makes wonderful miso soup, and there's plenty of seaweed in Seattle to use for it."

"I would enjoy that. In exchange I can teach her how to make bratwurst and sauerkraut."

Yoshiko scrunched up her face. "That's the stuff made from cabbage, right?"

Mama nodded.

Yoshiko's face broke into a grin. Soon Isabel joined the

laugher, and Mama, too. The idea of Mrs. Wakamutsu, in her traditional Japanese clothes, cooking sauerkraut created a hilarious picture.

"I learned the Japanese tea ceremony today," Isabel said.

"Show me!" Mama responded.

"We don't have any green matcha tea," Isabel said.

"We'll pretend with coffee," Mama said. She poured the coffee into a mug.

"No, Mama, it has to be in a cup with no handles."

"How about a bowl?" Mama glanced at Yoshiko.

"Yes, we could use a bowl," Yoshiko said.

Mama poured the coffee from the mug to a bowl and handed it to Yoshiko.

Yoshiko and Isabel spaced themselves a few feet apart on the kitchen floor and put the coffee between them. On her knees, Yoshiko bowed and offered the coffee to Isabel. Isabel bowed slowly then took the bowl carefully in her right hand. Then she moved it to her left hand and turned it around clockwise three times. Finally, she took a sip, wiped the cup, and returned it to Yoshiko.

Mama applauded. "Perfect. Next time we'll do it with the proper tea."

The apartment door creaked open.

"That must be your father," Mama said, filling another pan with water to boil the noodles.

Isabel heard Daddy murmur a greeting to Steven before coming into the kitchen.

At the sight of their father, the twins squirmed in the girls' arms. As soon as their feet hit the floor, they hurtled themselves toward Daddy and wrapped themselves around his legs. Isabel waited for the jovial greeting Daddy always gave the twins. But it did not come.

"Donald?" Mama said. "Are you all right?"

He sank into a chair and laid his newspaper on the table. "Donald?"

Isabel waited, holding her breath, for her father to say something.

"An army pilot tested the 299 in Ohio today," he said quietly.

"But that's good news," Isabel said.

Daddy shook his head. "They went over the plane inch by inch for weeks. They couldn't find anything wrong with it."

Isabel had a knot in her stomach. "Daddy, what happened?"

"Somebody made a mistake. The controls were left in the locked position."

"But that means—"

Daddy nodded. "That's right. The pilot had no control over the rudder or the flaps. He couldn't maneuver the plane."

"It crashed?" Isabel asked quietly.

Daddy nodded again. "The army pilot was killed. And the Boeing pilot on board was burned so badly that he'll probably die, too."

Mama's busy hands came to a stop. "Oh, Donald, I'm so sorry."

Steven pushed open the door to the kitchen and stopped in his tracks. "What happened?"

Isabel explained. Steven's shoulders sagged as he sighed.

Daddy reached for the paper and held it out to Steven. "Is this what you came in for?"

"Yes, I was going to check the scores."

"You might as well go ahead," Daddy said. "There's nothing to be done about the accident."

Steven opened the paper and started to flip to the sports section. "Oh, no."

"What is it?" everyone wanted to know.

"Italy has invaded Ethiopia."

Daddy groaned. Mama nervously turned back to her pots and pans.

"But Ethiopia isn't even in Europe," Isabel said. "It's in Africa. Why would Italy do that?"

"It's hard to explain."

"You always say that," Isabel protested.

"Because it's true."

"Japan, Germany, Italy—why can't everyone just be happy with the land they have?"

"I'm afraid it's more complicated than that," Daddy said, glancing at his German wife and Japanese neighbor. "It's clear that the political problems in Europe are going to affect the rest of the world."

"Isn't Mr. Martello Italian?" Isabel asked.

"Who is Mr. Martello?" Daddy asked.

"The vegetable man," Mama explained. "He has taken a liking to Alice and gives her a discount." Turning to Isabel, she said, "Yes, he is Italian."

"I wonder what he thinks about all this," Steven said.

Yoshiko had been listening quietly to the Harrington family conversation. "I should go now," she said. "My mother will be looking for me."

She backed toward the door with tiny steps and gave a traditional bow. No one smiled.

Mama poured the rice into the boiling water. "Isabel, go look for Frank and Audrey, please. I think they're in the apartment downstairs. Alice will be home soon, and we'll have supper."

Isabel dragged her feet down the stairs to the apartment on the third floor. Frank and Audrey were too young to care about what went on in Italy or Japan or anywhere else. They were lucky, Isabel thought.

CHAPTER 18
The Promise

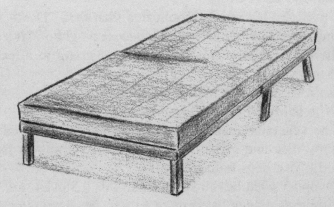

"Alice thinks we're silly for sitting out here like this," Isabel said. She closed her heavy jacket more snugly and crossed her arms across her chest. The cold air was starting to make her nose run.

"Don't take Alice too seriously," Steven replied. "She thinks she's a grown-up, so whatever we do, it's silly."

"You act like that sometimes, too, you know," Isabel informed her brother.

"Then don't take me too seriously, either."

"You have to learn to have more fun," Isabel declared.

Steven looked at her sideways. "Like the kind of fun you have when you tease poor Frank?"

"I don't ever do anything to hurt him."

They sat side by side on the front stoop in the late afternoon. In the fine days of summer, they had formed the habit of waiting for their father to come home at six o'clock every afternoon. If he did not come home in time for supper, they ate quickly and went back out to wait for him when he came home at eight o'clock.

As the seasons changed and the weather cooled, they did not change their habit. It was early December, and the gray afternoons were nippy and sometimes wet. But Steven and Isabel faithfully waited on the stoop.

All summer and into the fall, the neighborhood had buzzed. Girls, including Yoshiko and Isabel, hopscotched on the sidewalks, while their brothers, including Steven, Frank, and Kaneko, tossed baseballs around. Mr. Wakamutsu had come out twice a day in his white apron to sweep the sidewalk around the entrance to his building. In the hottest days of August, the children squirted each other with a hose.

Isabel and Steven had gotten to know the neighbors from their own building, as well as dozens of people from the buildings around them. Someone was always outside doing something, and it was easy to strike up a conversation.

September had come, and the children had gone back to school, including the Harrington children. Not much of the afternoon was left by the time they got home, but they took advantage of even an hour to be outside before suppertime.

As the fall deepened, mothers called out reminders to their children to wear jackets and keep their shoes on. The afternoons turned gray, and the sun seemed hardly half as strong as it was in the summer. Seattle's reputation for being a rainy city proved true. Afternoon clouds hovered over the neighborhood and burst open on a daily basis. Occasionally the moisture came in the form of wet snowflakes.

"She might be right, you know," Isabel said.

"Who?"

"Alice. It is pretty cold out here."

"If you're cold, you can go inside," Steven said.

"I didn't say that."

"Suit yourself."

They turned their heads in the direction Daddy would come from.

"Do you think he'll find a paper on the streetcar today?" Isabel asked.

Steven shrugged. "He always comes home with one. I think he buys it now."

Isabel nodded. "Me, too. It's always the *Post Intelligencer.* Never the *Times.*"

"He knows I like the sports section in the *P-I.*"

Isabel was silent for a few minutes. Then she said, "Steven, are you glad we came to Seattle?"

Steven turned to face her. "Why do you ask a question like that?"

"I'm just wondering. Are you glad?"

He shrugged. "I miss some things about Minneapolis. But in Minneapolis, it would really be too cold to sit outside and wait for Daddy."

"Not that kind of stuff," Isabel said. "The weather doesn't matter to me."

"What do you think?" Steven turned the question back to his sister. "Are you glad to be in Seattle?"

"It feels far away."

"It is far away from Minneapolis."

"But at least we're still in the United States. All those countries in Europe are so small and smushed up against each other."

Steven smiled. "Imagine that someone in Germany drove as long as we did when we moved out here. No telling where they'd end up."

"I'm kind of glad I didn't have to go to Japan to meet some Japanese people," Isabel said, "and I didn't have to go to Italy to meet somebody like Mr. Martello."

"Yoshiko has turned out to be a very good friend for you," Steven observed.

Isabel nodded her agreement. "Oh, look. Here she comes now."

Yoshiko and her brother Kaneko were trudging up the block with their arms full of grocery sacks. Isabel hopped off the stoop and walked through the slush to meet them. She took a sack from Yoshiko's arms.

"Thank you, Isabel. I was afraid I was about to drop that one." Yoshiko glanced at her brother to make sure he still had a good grip on his sack.

When they reached the stoop, Steven stood up to open the door. "You have quite a load there."

Yoshiko nodded her head briefly to acknowledge Steven's politeness.

"I'm going to help her carry these things in," Isabel informed her brother.

To get to the Wakamutsu apartment, they had to cross the main lobby of the hotel portion of the building. Mr. Wakamutsu was behind the reception desk working on some papers. He glanced up briefly and smiled as they passed. As always, the lobby was spotlessly clean. Every chair was in place, every lamp dusted, every scrap of paper removed, and the white walls scrubbed clean.

They entered the Wakamutsu apartment. It was a double-size apartment. Mr. Wakamutsu had taken out a wall between two units to accommodate his family. Only five people lived in seven rooms. To Isabel, it seemed luxurious. All nine Harringtons lived in only four rooms. The boys slept in the living room every night. Yoshiko had her own room. Isabel could hardly imagine having her own bed, much less her own room.

Even with their arms full, Yoshiko and Kaneko paused to slip off their shoes before walking through the apartment. Isabel did the same. It may have been a Japanese custom, but she thought it made a lot of sense not to wear shoes in the house, especially wet ones.

The decorating scheme of the Wakamutsu apartment was an odd mixture of traditional Japanese art and furniture blended with some functional American-style furniture. The Wakamutsus slept on beds low to the floor. But they chose to eat their meals at a wooden table purchased at a local department store rather than sitting on the floor in traditional fashion.

The layout of the kitchen was identical to the Harringtons'. Isabel felt like she ought to know her way around the Wakamutsu kitchen. But, of course, everything was kept in different places than the way the Harrington kitchen was arranged.

They set the grocery sacks on the counter with relief. Kaneko immediately disappeared.

"He always thinks the work is done when we get home from the store," Yoshiko said. She began unpacking a sack.

"That's okay," Isabel said. "I can help." She reached into another sack and pulled out a heavy bag of rice. There wasn't much else left in the outer sack. "This is the biggest bag of rice I've ever seen!"

Yoshiko grinned. "We eat a lot of rice. That's the Japanese way."

140

"What else do you have in these sacks?"

"Tofu, eggs for custard, soy sauce, soybeans, all the usual stuff."

Isabel chuckled. "Your grocery list is a lot different than ours."

"It's just food."

"Yoshiko," Isabel said, "what if you could never eat rice again?"

"Huh? Why wouldn't I be able to eat rice?"

"I don't know why. But just suppose you couldn't. You would still be you, right?"

Yoshiko set a jug of milk on the counter. "I'm not sure what you're talking about."

"What if you couldn't do things the Japanese way?" Isabel continued. "Would that bother you?"

Yoshiko thought for a second. "I hated going to Japanese school when I started. But now I think it's kind of fun to understand the culture my parents came from. But I know the Japanese way is not the only way."

"So you would still be you, even if you weren't Japanese."

"But I am Japanese."

"I thought you considered yourself an American."

"I do. But I'm Japanese, too."

"I'm getting confused," Isabel said.

"You're the one who started talking about all this," Yoshiko reminded her.

"Well, I just wanted to say that I would like you and want you for my friend no matter what country your parents came from. I wouldn't care what kind of food you ate, or what strange traditions you had, or whether or not you followed them."

Yoshiko looked at her friend. "I am not ashamed to be

141

Japanese," Yoshiko said slowly, "and you should not be ashamed to be part German."

"I'm not!"

"Just remember that."

"Do you know what, Yoshiko, all of life is an adventure."

"I thought we were talking about cultures."

"We are. When we moved from Minneapolis to Seattle, my mother said it was a grand adventure of faith. We didn't know what we would find when we got here or what our life would be like. I'm just glad that I found you here."

"And I'm glad you came."

"So I hope I can keep having adventures. Who knows what other surprises I'll have."

"Isabel Harrington, you are thinking very deep thoughts today," Yoshiko said. She put the milk in the icebox.

Isabel chuckled. "Nobody expects that from me."

"I like it."

"I have one more serious thing to say."

"Okay, what is it?"

"I, Isabel Harrington, promise to be a loyal friend to Yoshiko Wakamutsu for as long as I live."

Yoshiko stared at Isabel for a moment. "That is serious."

"Well?"

Yoshiko sucked in her breath. "I, Yoshiko Wakamutsu, promise to be a loyal friend to Isabel Harrington for as long as I live."

"There," Isabel said with satisfaction. "I don't care what happens in Europe or anywhere else in the world." She picked up the bag of rice. "Now when do I get to learn how to use that Japanese rice cooker?"

There's More!

The American Adventure continues with *Changing Times*. Frank and Isabel are horrified to see two men attack their father as he walks home from work, carrying Christmas presents. Why would people be desperate enough to steal someone else's gifts?

Soon the Harringtons and Wakamutsus are busy carrying out Frank's plan to help the homeless men in their neighborhood. But Isabel still finds plenty of time to pull pranks on her younger brother. Then one of her pranks turns dangerous. She and Frank are lost on Mt. Rainier. How will they be rescued? When will Frank learn to think for himself? And will Isabel ever be as bothered by the way she treats Frank as she is by how others treat her friends, the Wakamutsus?

You're in for the ultimate
American Adventure!
Collect all 48 books!